Dog of Thieves

A Golden Retriever Mystery

Neil S. Plakcy

Samwise Books

Contents

Reviews

Mr. Plakcy did a terrific job in this cozy mystery. He has a smooth writing style that kept the story flowing evenly. The dialogue and descriptions were right on target.

Book Blogger Red Adept

Steve and Rochester become quite a team and Neil Plakcy is the kind of writer that I want to tell me this story. It's a fun read which will keep you turning pages very quickly.

Amazon top 100 reviewer Amos Lassen

In Dog We Trust is a very well-crafted mystery that kept me guessing up until Steve figured out where things were going.

E-book addict reviews

Neil Plakcy's golden retriever mysteries are supposed to be about former computer hacker Steve Levitan, but it is his golden retriever

Rochester who is the real amateur sleuth in this delightful academic mystery. This is no talking dog book, though. Rochester doesn't need anything more than his wagging tail and doggy smile to win over readers and help solve crimes. I absolutely fell in love with this brilliant dog who digs up clues and points the silly humans towards the evidence.

– Christine Kling, author of *Circle of Bones*.

Chapter 1

Trouble with Trees

T he early morning sun glinted off Rochester's golden fur as he sniffed something. When he lifted his head, his snout quivered with the joy of whatever it was he'd inhaled. It was garbage day, and in the distance I heard the blast of the truck's horn, notifying someone who'd parked on one of River Bend's narrow streets that the truck was blocked. A thirty-something guy with a messenger bag over his shoulder zipped past us on a scooter, and Rochester looked up at me and blinked several times.

As he lifted his leg against one of the magnificent oaks that line our street, I noticed a splotch of rust-red paint the color of dried blood on the center of the trunk.

Somewhere other than in our gated community, it might have been a sign of vandalism, a gang tag, or a signature by a graffiti artist. Instead, it was the mark of death for the poor tree.

Some twenty-five years ago, when River Bend was built, the developer planted hundreds of oak saplings along our narrow, winding streets. Sadly, no one had thought to consider the future of those trees, which began spreading roots as they grew taller. Now,

1

those knobby roots were pushing up concrete pavers in driveways and tearing through the paved streets.

While Rochester was peeing, I saw a familiar neighbor approaching on a three-wheeled bicycle. Pete Szabo had moved into a townhouse on Bucharest Place earlier that year and had already gained a reputation as a troublemaker. I tugged Rochester forward, hoping to dart through the gap between townhouse blocks and avoid speaking to Pete, but no such luck.

"That arborist the association hired is a clueless idiot," he said, in lieu of a greeting, as he braked his bike beside me.

The problem with the trees had gotten so bad that a year before River Bend had commissioned a tree-removal company to examine all the oaks and decide which ones should be taken out. The home-owners' association had assessed us all, and promised that the oaks would be replaced with new trees planted a safer distance from anywhere they could cause damage.

"Good morning, Pete. It's not an easy task," I said. "Remember, we're a zero-lot-line community and our driveways were already at the minimum width. Our house doesn't have much of a front yard so there won't be a lot of room to relocate a tree." We had a concrete-walled courtyard lined with the same pavers as the driveway and only a six-by-ten patch of grass and landscaping in front of that.

"I don't have a problem," he said. "My tree is far enough back from the street. I resent having to pay for other peoples' trees to be removed. And one of the reasons I bought here was the tree canopy. I don't want to lose that."

"I know what you mean," I said, as Rochester settled on the pave-ment beside me. Whenever I want him to pull me forward, he plops his butt like that. "I depend on the shade to walk Rochester on hot summer days, and I'm not happy about losing trees either."

"You're on the tree removal committee, aren't you? When are they going to start cutting the trees down?"

"The blood-red splotches are a sign that the removal is going to happen soon," I said. "We signed a contract last week with a company and gave them a down payment."

He frowned. "We'll see if it happens," he said, and he cycled past us.

Even though it was March 15, I was sweaty by the time we got back home and I worried that I'd feel even worse once the trees came down and summer arrived.

As soon as I opened the front door, I heard my fiancée Lili calling from upstairs. "Steve! I've been waiting for you to get back. I have to leave."

"I had a key with me," I called, as I unhooked Rochester's leash. "You could have left."

"I didn't know."

She came downstairs in a rush, pulling her auburn curls back behind her head into a makeshift ponytail.

"You could have noticed that the front door was locked," I said. "That means I locked it from the outside."

"I am not the detective in this family," she said. "And Rochester wasn't here to point that out."

"Ah, a subtle dig," I said, smiling. I kissed her cheek. Rochester had gained a reputation as a clue-sniffing dog, and I usually trailed along behind him, putting those clues together to solve whatever mystery faced us, from murder to where Lili had left her phone.

"I have a meeting of all the department heads at nine," she said. "I don't want to be the last one in the room."

Lili was the chair of the Department of Fine Arts at Eastern College, where I also worked, as the administrator of a conference center called Friar Lake. She grabbed her purse and a leather portfolio of student work she was grading for the course she was teaching, and she was out the door.

I had more time, so I poured Rochester his breakfast kibble and plated up a chocolate chip muffin for my breakfast. In my defense, it had some oat flour in it, so it wasn't a total calorie bomb.

Rochester ate noisily while I checked my email. I deleted all the spam about class action suits for non-Hodgkin's lymphoma and cancer caused by drinking the water at Camp Lejeune, the offers to show me African tricks to increase my sexual performance and Tommy Chong's CBD gummies.

Rochester heard the gate open at the same time I did, and he jumped up and rushed to the front door, barking. I looked through the sliding glass door, expecting to see a delivery, but instead spotted Jennifer Dodge, the chair of the tree removal committee.

She looked like she was on her way to a coffee-shop rendezvous, in a black T-shirt and skinny black jeans. Her blonde hair fell in straight lines almost all the way to her waist. I hurried over to the door.

"Hey, Jennifer," I said. I grabbed hold of Rochester's collar to keep him from jumping on her and covering her slacks with golden hair.

"Sorry to bother you, but I saw your car in the driveway. Do you have a couple of minutes?"

"Sure. I'm my own boss, so I don't have to punch a time clock. Come on in."

I let go of Rochester's collar and stepped back. "Be nice," I said to him.

She reached down to pet him. "He's such a beautiful dog," she said. "I see you walking him and I want to take a picture for my Instagram."

She followed me into the kitchen. "Can I offer you a coffee, water, something?"

She shook her head. "We have a real problem with Tree-B-Gone and I was hoping you could help."

We sat across from each other and Rochester sprawled on the floor beside me. "What's the problem?"

"I called Vic Davis's personal cell this morning to confirm when he's going to start removing trees." She took a deep breath. "I got a message that said that the number I had reached was no longer in service."

I nodded. "And?"

"I knew the office opens at eight-thirty, so I called that number. The secretary said that Vic emailed the employees early this morning that he was shutting the business down and there was no money to pay their salaries."

"Holy crap," I said, and I sat back against my chair.

Rochester rose from the floor and came to nuzzle my leg. I stroked behind his ears as Jennifer continued.

"I've notified the association's attorney. We paid Tree-B-Gone $100,000, and it looks like we'll have to track Davis down to find out how we get our money back. I know you have some computer skills and I was hoping you could help."

"I can try," I said. "Can you email me everything you know about his company? I'll see what I can find out."

"That would be great," she said. "My Internet knowledge is limited to finding yoga workout videos and ordering take-out."

"If you have a copy of the contract I'd like to see that, too," I said. "I've done some freelance writing in the past, and from that I know my way around a contract."

"I didn't sign the contract myself—Henry Meskin did." Henry was the chair of the board of directors for the homeowners association.

"All right. I'll see if I can track down Vic Davis. But I wouldn't get too upset right now. The HOA should have required a performance bond before signing the contract, and that should protect us."

"What's a performance bond?"

"It's a bond provided by a bank or insurance company to ensure that the contractor meets his obligations," I said.

"Interesting. I've never heard that term before. But like I said, Henry handled all the final dealings with Tree-B-Gone. I only interviewed the contractors. Tree-B-Gone came highly recommended by one of the homeowners, and they gave us the best price."

"Do you remember who recommended them?"

She shook her head. "I've tried. But it wasn't anything in writing.

I was out looking at trees and someone came up and we got into a conversation. I'm pretty sure it was a woman, and she said that she knew about Tree-B-Gone and we should use them."

"If you remember anything more, let me know. In the meantime I'll see what I can find."

She stood up. "Thanks, Steve. I'm dreading having to notify the HOA about this. I'm hoping we'll find a way out."

As I walked her to the door, I remembered a similar situation that had come up when I was freelancing. One of my clients was a urologist with a law degree, who had started a side gig training people at the intersection of medicine and law. He had developed courses for legal nurse consultants and health care risk managers, and I wrote the copy for his promotional brochures. He'd run out on his business in the same way, avoiding alimony and losses on his business.

History was repeating itself. I'd only lost a thousand dollars when the doctor stiffed me, but now the homeowners association was going to be out a hundred grand—some of which had come out of my pocket.

Could I track down Vic Davis and help the association get our money back? It was the kind of challenge that made my fingers itch to get onto the special laptop I kept for my occasional forays into hacking.

Rochester trailed me as I hurried to the garage, where I retrieved my ladder. Then he was underfoot as I carried it upstairs. I positioned it in front of the air handler and climbed up, pushing aside the ceiling panel that led to the attic. I groped around for a minute and found the laptop, which I kept up there out of sight, so that I had to make a real effort to get it and use it.

This situation called for that kind of desperate measure. I grabbed the laptop and replaced the panel, then put the ladder back in the garage, all the while with Rochester underfoot. By then I was running late, so I took a quick shower and dressed. Rochester rode shotgun beside me as we headed up River Road from Stewart's

Crossing to the hilly country lane that would take us up to Friar Lake.

I had a lot on my plate that day, but I knew I'd make some time to hunt up information on Vic Davis and Tree-B-Gone. Otherwise it would be money-b-gone for the River Bend homeowners association.

Chapter 2

Doggie Demo

Like Lili, I had a busy day ahead of me. Spring break would be upon us soon, and Friar Lake was booked up with class visits, invited speakers, and community meetings. Originally called Our Lady of the Waters, the property had been owned by an order of monks who had lacked the funds to keep it up. Eastern had bought the property three years before, and I'd been hired to oversee the renovation and then manage it.

It was a great job for me, because I could bring Rochester to work with me every day. I called him my Velcro dog, and he was happiest when he had me in his sights, or was sleeping beside me. I also considered myself a jack of all trades, master of none. I knew a few things about many topics, which helped me set up programming at Friar Lake, and running the facility was different every day.

That morning, biology professor Fred Searcy was bringing a class to identify wild and domesticated plants on our acreage. The local Realtors association was having a lunchtime meeting, and then the women's lacrosse team was coming up to us to practice while their campus field was being renovated.

As I pulled into the parking space in front of the restored carriage house where I had my office, I saw my counterpart, Joey Capodilupo, climbing up a ladder against a huge maple tree beside the old chapel.

Joey managed the physical plant operations of the center, supervising outside contractors as well as his own lawn crew, and handling minor repairs. There was always something going wrong with one of the two-hundred-year-old buildings, and one of us was always there when the facility was in use.

Joey was holding what my father used to call a pair of extension loppers. I didn't know the official name for them, but they had long handles and a wicked blade attached to a string. My father used them to chop off high branches, which was what Joey was trying to do.

It was strange that I had so many tree-related things going on, but that was spring in Pennsylvania. The weeping willows down by the lakefront were leaning farther down toward the water, the oaks and sycamores were sending off new shoots, and the apple trees were blossoming.

One of the big branches of the maple had broken in a strong wind we'd had a few weeks before, and it hung at a strange angle. I jumped out of the car and hurried over to hold the ladder for Joey as he climbed higher, trying to get purchase on that dead limb.

"Thanks," he called down. "I want to get this branch off before the tree goes into leaf. It'll be harder to get to it then."

Rochester sprawled on the ground beside me as I watched Joey grapple for the branch. He finally got hold of it and pulled the rope to slice it off. It came tumbling down, startling Rochester, who jumped up. As soon as it was on the ground, though, he was sniffing it, and before Joey had even climbed down the ladder Rochester had anointed the branch.

"That was trouble," he said, as he reached the ground. "See how thick it is? But I'll cut it down and it'll make good kindling."

"Isn't it still too green?"

"I'm planning for next winter," Joey said. He was a big, cheerful guy, a few inches over six feet and built like a lumberjack. "Mark and

I have used up almost all the wood I put aside last year. You have to get a head start if you want to stay warm."

Joey and his partner Mark had bought a townhouse in River Bend the year before, and Joey, who was handy at everything, was gradually renovating and modifying it. I wished I had his skills—my father had been good at building and repairing, but the gene had skipped me. When things went wrong at our townhouse, either Lili or I bumbled through fixing it, or we called Joey or a repair company.

I left him to chop the limb and Rochester and I went into my office in the gatehouse, where he settled down by the wall and took a nap. Though I really wanted to pull out the hacker laptop and look for information on Vic Davis, I logged into my office computer and began reading and answering college emails.

The most interesting one was from Ewan Stone, a professor of philosophy I had come to know because we'd been on several committees together. He wanted to invite a history professor from the University of Pennsylvania to come up to Friar Lake and demonstrate how a dog could be trained to sniff out historical artifacts.

He'd listed his office hours at the bottom of the email, so I could see when it was a good time to call him. I dialed his four-digit college extension, and he answered quickly. "Hey, Steve, thanks for getting back to me."

"Tell me about this professor you want to invite."

"I took a history course with him when I was getting my PhD," he said. "And I've been following his latest gig. He's collaborating with the Working Dog Center at Penn to train scent dogs to check luggage for stolen artifacts."

Anything to do with dogs perked up my interest. "Scent dogs?"

"Dogs have up to 300 million olfactory receptors in their noses, compared to about six million in us. And the part of a dog's brain that is devoted to analyzing smells is about 40 times greater than ours. So they can be trained to sniff out drugs, to tell if an epileptic is about to have a seizure, even to alert if someone has cancer. They've been used at airports for a long time to find drugs."

I heard him stop for a moment to drink something.

"There's a big trade in smuggled artifacts coming out of the Fertile Crescent," he continued. "Particularly Iraq and Syria, because of all the violence there, the poverty, and the presence of modern-day bandits. Professor Suleiman had this idea to work with the museum and the dog center to see if dogs could be trained to sniff these artifacts."

"That's very cool."

"I asked him if he'd be willing to come up to Eastern with the handler who's training the dogs and give a demonstration, and he agreed. I thought Friar Lake would be the perfect place for it."

"I agree. Fill out a facilities request with the day and time you want to hold the event and I'll get on it."

Rochester looked up at me when I ended the call. "What do you think, puppy? You're a clue-sniffing dog. Think you could be trained to find stolen artifacts?"

He opened his mouth wide and yawned. I laughed. "I guess not, then."

The day passed quickly and it wasn't until after Fred's class had left, the Realtors had completed their luncheon, and the women's lacrosse team was engaged in their practice that I had the chance to go back to my personal emails, where I found a message from Jennifer Dodge, reminding us that there was a meeting of the board of directors that evening at the clubhouse, and tree removal was on the agenda.

"In light of what's happened with Tree-B-Gone I need the whole committee there to back me up," she wrote. "Please do your best to attend."

As soon as I saw that, I grabbed my hacker laptop to look for information on Vic Davis and Tree-B-Gone.

The materials she had emailed me personally indicated that she had solicited bids from several contractors, and Tree-B-Gone came in with the lowest number – but not significantly lower than the others to make us suspicious. According to the company's website, Davis was certified by the International Society of Arboriculture and had decades of experience in assessing and removing trees.

The other members of the committee and I had gone along with Jennifer's recommendation. Hey, it was our money, and we wanted to spend as little of it as possible.

I did what I should have done before we signed the contract. I went to the ISA website to verify Vic's credentials – and no surprise, he wasn't listed there. So I called the ISA office in Atlanta.

"My homeowners association is interested in hiring an arborist, and he says that he's been certified by your organization, but I can't find him listed on your website. Can you tell me anything about him or his company?"

I gave her Vic's name and the address of Tree-B-Gone, and heard her fingers on a keyboard. "I don't have anything in our records on him," she said after a moment. "I can't say anything official, but often individuals will cite us in their publicity materials when they don't actually have the training."

I thanked her. Things were not looking good.

I scooted my chair over to the credenza where I'd left my hacker laptop. Rochester woke up and stared at me as I rolled back to my desk and opened the laptop. "Don't worry, buddy. I'm not doing anything wrong. Just snooping."

I did some digging in some databases I had access to, including ones that tracked criminal records. Sure enough, Victor Davis showed up. He had been charged with credit card fraud from a previous business in New Jersey. According to the police report, he had set up a website where he listed items he had bought from department stores selling off old inventory by the pallet.

Unfortunately, he didn't have many of the items, and customers began placing complaints with their credit card companies. Eventually he'd declared bankruptcy and shut down his business.

How had he ended up running a tree-trimming operation? And why had we hired him?

I heard a hard rap on the door to the gatehouse, and I quickly shut the lid on the hacker laptop. Joey stuck his head in the door and I was relieved. "Need your help," he said. "The lacrosse team broke one of the portable goals. Can you give me and the coach a hand to get it back to his truck?"

The orange posts of the goal were designed to fold in to make it easier to carry, but an errant ball had slammed into one side and it no longer folded. The young woman who'd thrown the ball joined the three of us in awkwardly carrying the posts, while other players carried the nets and related paraphernalia.

Even though a chill had set in, I was perspiring by the time I got back to my office, where I had to wrap everything up quickly to get home and make dinner.

Lili was already in the living room, scanning through something on her laptop. When I leaned in to kiss her cheek I saw she was surveying wedding venues.

Lili had accepted my proposal a couple of months before, but we hadn't announced our decision to anyone yet. We had both been through divorces, and though we had been together for a few years and were committed to each other, we hadn't made a formal announcement yet.

That was partly because we had different ideas about what kind of wedding we wanted. I left her looking, with Rochester settled beside her, and went into the kitchen. As I cooked, I remembered my very formal wedding to Mary, my first wife. The planning began months in advance, and included a big shower at a party venue near her parents' house on Long Island. Next up was an aufruf at Shomrei Torah in Trenton, where I'd been a bar mitzvah. Mary and I were called to the Torah for a blessing, and then the congregation wished us mazel tov and happiness by throwing soft candies at us.

I know, it's a weird tradition, but I kind of liked it. And the kids in the audience scampered around collecting the candy. We'd done it because it was part of the wedding, and even though my parents weren't that religious, they wanted to do something local for their friends and people who wouldn't be invited to the wedding.

I kept cooking as all the memories flooded back. I resisted having a bachelor party, because most of my groomsmen ended up being Mary's cousins, and I didn't know any of them that well. Instead, my graduate school roommate Tor served as my best man, and we went out for dinner together instead of having a party.

Mary and I were married at the synagogue in Roslyn where she had been a bat mitzvah, and where she had dreamed of walking up the long aisle between the pews in a formal white wedding gown.

As with most things in our marriage, Mary got what she wanted. She had five bridesmaids in pale pink gowns with broad-brimmed picture hats. Her parents paraded her down the aisle like a prize they were giving away. We didn't promise to obey each other, but Mary marched around me seven times, to create a magical wall of protection from evil spirits, temptation, and the glances of other women.

Her parents went all out for the reception. Guests were offered samplers of a custom Cosmopolitan with citron vodka rather than regular. Servers passed cocktail franks and tiny meatballs on skewers. Diners had a choice of filet mignon or salmon. And our wedding cake was four layers of chocolate cake with pink icing that matched the bridesmaids' dresses.

The cake topper should have told us everything. Mary had fallen in love with one in which a bride in a white gown held a butterfly net over a groom in a tuxedo.

As I plated up our Caesar salads with grilled chicken, I remembered the way Lili had described her weddings. She married her first husband while she was still in college, a simple trip to the New York City Marriage Bureau downtown. Then her second had been a brief ceremony in the apartment where she and her fiancé were living on the Upper East Side.

I wanted something simple, but Lili was longing for the kind of public commitment she felt was lacking in her previous marriages. So until we worked through those differences, we weren't going to tell anyone.

I brought the salads to the table and called Lili in. Of course I'd kept out a few pieces of chicken which I fed to Rochester as we ate. "How was your day?" she asked.

I told her what I had learned about Vic Davis and Tree-B-Gone. "You didn't hire him, did you?"

"The association did the hiring. The committee recommended him."

"And you're on the committee."

"Yes, and we certainly didn't do our due diligence before we signed the contract. I'm not trying to throw Jennifer Dodge under the bus, but she pushed to hire the company because they were the lowest bidder and she said that one of her neighbors highly recommended him."

"And you get what you pay for. Or in this case, you don't."

Chapter 3

Civic Duties

We ate quickly, so I could get to the association meeting on time, and I gave Rochester a shorter than usual walk. He gave me a sad face as I stepped around him to head out. A blustery March wind was sweeping down Sarajevo Way, so I drove over to the clubhouse and parked in the lot, which was already almost full.

I saw several neighbors I knew when I walked in, and I waved or nodded. They were other dog people, and I usually knew them only by their dogs' names. I sat beside Bob Freehl, a retired Stewart's Crossing cop who lived down the street from me. "Going to get ugly tonight," he said.

"How do you know?"

"I can read the room. Look over there, at that woman in the brown dress. See those fliers she's got in her hand? She tried to give me one of them when I walked in. Save the tree canopy."

He snorted. "What about save my driveway? The oak in front of my house has pushed up the pavers and the street asphalt is all cracked. Every time I go in and out of my driveway I'm afraid I'm going to puncture a tire. And I can't do anything about it because River Bend controls the street maintenance."

I recognized the woman he was pointing to. Mary Kate Donahue was a Realtor who listed a lot of homes in River Bend, and one of the selling points she made was how beautiful the neighborhood was with all the trees lining the streets.

"Then look over to the other side," Bob said. "That old geezer who looks like he knew God in short pants? That's Arnold Lafoon. He tripped and fell over a bubble in the pavement and he's threatening to sue the association if they don't tear up the trees and fix the roads while he's still got enough strength to walk."

Most of our board of directors were new; we'd had a scandal a year before involving the landscape contractor, and several of the homeowners on that board had been forced to resign. I hoped this crew would be more honest.

But I couldn't imagine what they would say when they heard about the problems with Tree-B-Gone. Over in the corner I saw the trike-rider, Pete Szabo, talking with Jennifer Dodge.

The new president, Henry Meskin, called the meeting to order. He was an electrical engineer and had run a trade association, which made him a strict parliamentarian. He insisted on reading the minutes of the previous meeting and having them approved. Then he went through a list of items in order, with the report from the tree committee scheduled for last.

The natives were getting restless as he went over budget items for repairing the pool pump, adding a new light fixture, and approving the payments for various contractors who had worked at the community since the last meeting.

He finally called for the tree committee's report. Jennifer stood up. "We got some bad news this morning," she said. "The arborist we hired, who completed the survey last week and was supposed to begin tree removal next week, has shut down his company and disappeared."

There was a rumble in the room as people turned to their neighbors to express their surprise. Henry banged his gavel. "Quiet, everyone. Jennifer, where does this leave us?"

She shrugged. "I only found out this morning. I notified the association's attorney, and he's going to investigate any recourse we have."

"What kind of progress have you made on actually getting the trees removed?"

Jennifer looked pretty upset, so I raised my hand. Because I was tall and had a big, booming voice, I had been nominated by the committee to deliver our recommendations in the past.

I stood up and made my way to the front of the room. "I'm Steve Levitan, and I live on Seagrape Way," I began. "Many of you might recognize me because I'm out walking my golden retriever regularly. That's why I asked to serve on this committee—because maintaining the tree canopy is important to me, especially in the summer, when I appreciate the shade."

"Hear, hear!" Mary Kate called.

Henry banged his ceremonial gavel on the table in front of him. "Quiet in the room!"

There was grumbling among Mary Kate's cohort but Henry glared at them and wouldn't let me continue until they were quiet.

"There are six members on our committee, and at least one of us has reviewed every oak tree in River Bend. There are 458 of them, in case you were curious."

"Soon to be a lot fewer," Arnold Lafoon called.

"Shut up, Arnold," Henry said. "You'll have your time to talk when we open the floor."

"Ought to open a trap door in the floor and push you through," Arnold grumbled.

Henry had his mouth open to say something further when I interrupted. "Sorry, our studies have revealed that the water table is too high in River Bend for trap doors," I said, and the audience laughed, though both Henry and Arnold glared at me.

"The committee will now pass around copies of our survey," I said, as my fellow members stood up and began handing out sheets of paper. I had surreptitiously done all the copying at Friar Lake. I figured it was a community service.

"You'll see each street labeled, and each oak tree identified. If the tree has a star, that means it is far enough back from streets and driveways not to be a danger." I looked at Arnold. "We don't want anyone tripping over roots, and we want to be able to repave the streets this summer, so any tree that has torn up the street near it has an X."

The room was quiet as everyone bent their heads to examine the map for their street and the trees near them.

"Finally, there are some trees that aren't disturbing the street, but are damaging homeowner driveways. We've marked those with a circle. As you know, we're a zero-lot-line community, so our houses are very close to each other. It's possible that a tree on my property may be damaging my next-door neighbor's driveway. We're asking those neighbors who are affected to talk directly to each other and let the association know if they both agree to have the tree removed, or leave it in place."

"What if they disagree?"

The woman who asked the question was white-haired and had a tiny, very barky West Highland White Terrier whose hair matched hers. I looked at Henry, who nodded slightly. I had seen her around River Bend, and knew that her name was Malgorzata Stopnicki. She spoke with a heavy accent, so I assumed she was an immigrant from somewhere in Eastern Europe, probably Poland.

"If there is a disagreement between neighbors, then the owner of the property has the final say," I said. "Fortunately there are only six trees in that situation."

Mary Kate raised her hand. "By my calculation, you're removing over a hundred fifty trees!" she said. "Do you all know what that's going to do to property values?"

"Every tree that is removed will be replaced by a sapling, planted safely away from streets and driveways," I said. "The committee has selected three different types of maples that have non-invasive root systems, as well as the Chinese pistache and the red tip photinia. If a sapling is to be planted on your property, you'll get to choose which one you want."

"Some of these trees can take ten years to grow!" a man in a business suit pointed out. "I plan to sell my house long before that happens."

"I might not even have ten years left," Arnold Laffoon said.

"Widening the variety of trees in the community will enhance property values in the long run," I added. "We've all seen that summers are getting hotter and drier, so replacing a lot of the oaks with these other trees means we'll be less likely to have problems in the future."

I paused, then added, "Of course, now the program will be delayed while we find a new company."

"What about our money?" Arnold demanded. "How are we going to get that back?"

"I can't speak to that. I did some research on Vic Davis and Tree-B-Gone today, though, and I have to say I doubt we'll get any of it. He's already declared bankruptcy for a business in New Jersey and he has a number of judgments against him there."

"How come you didn't know that before we hired him?" Arnold again.

"We didn't do a criminal records check before we hired him. Maybe we should have. The tree committee passed our recommendation to the board and Catalina, the property manager. I think the board depends on guidance from her before signing anything."

People began arguing and speaking over each other, and no matter how many times Henry banged his gavel he couldn't get quiet. "Meeting adjourned!" he roared eventually, and the board got up from their seats.

Henry managed to slip out, but I was besieged by angry neighbors and Malgorzata tried to hit me with her cane to get me to pay attention to her, and I turned at her and glared. "You hit me with that cane, lady, and I'll have you arrested for assault before you can say stool softener," I said.

Someone else started to yell, and I said, in my loudest voice, "We're all neighbors here, and the members of the tree committee are volunteers. If you can't talk in a normal voice then I'm out of here."

That had no effect. I wished I'd brought Rochester along—he could have cleared an exit path for me. But instead I looked pleadingly at Bob Freehl, who stood against one wall. He shrugged and held his arm out. "Shut up, everyone. I may be a retired cop but I can still have any of you arrested for disturbing the peace."

That made people turn to look at him, and I was able to nudge my way through the clot of neighbors until I reached the front door and made my escape.

So much for my civic duties, I thought. Lili was right when she'd told me to stay out of this business.

Chapter 4

Stolen Artifacts

By the time I got home I was in no mood to keep searching for information on Vic Davis. That could wait until the next day. I filled Lili in on what had happened at the meeting. "It was a mess. But we can't move forward until we figure out what happened to Vic Davis and Tree-B-Gone."

"I noticed your hacker laptop on the dining room table. Are you going to search for him?"

"I'll see what I can find, legally," I said. "To give the association attorney a head start."

She leaned over and kissed my cheek. "Try to stay out of trouble, please."

"I will."

I noticed that I'd agreed to "try" to stay out of trouble. I'd have to do better than that.

Lili had queued up a movie for us to watch on our streaming service, so we watched *Ocean's Eleven*, a George Clooney movie we'd missed when it came to the theaters. As soon as I realized that the story began with the Clooney character released from prison, I was all in. It was easy to project my own experience onto a handsome and dapper actor.

Of course, I didn't start planning a new crime as soon as I was set free, as Clooney did. I was too traumatized by my time inside and all the things that had happened while I was locked up. My wife had filed for a divorce and stowed my few personal items in a storage locker. My father had died and left me the townhouse in Stewart's Crossing.

And I was still struggling to get over the issue that had sent me to prison in the first place—my wife's miscarriages.

But I connected with the first two parts of Clooney's mantra: Don't hurt anybody, don't steal from anyone who doesn't deserve it, and play the game like you've got nothing to lose. Back then I felt like I had lost everything that mattered to me. Now, with Rochester's help, I had built a new life. I had Lili's love, a roof over our heads, and a satisfying career. Too bad I still had the itch to stick my nose into places online where it didn't belong. I couldn't keep playing the game like I had nothing to lose, because I had so much.

Lili leaned in against me as Clooney's gang worked their magic, and Rochester snoozed at my feet. I realized that Lili was dozing, too, but I had to know how the movie ended. Would Clooney's character get away with everything?

Lili woke up as the credits rolled. "What happened?" she asked with a yawn.

"I didn't like the ending," I said. "Clooney returned to prison for violating his parole, and his ex-wife went back to him."

"Well, your ending was better," she said. "You've managed to stay out of prison, despite a few close calls."

"And I have no desire to get back together with Mary," I said. "I'm much happier to have found you."

"So much for Hollywood endings," she said. Both she and Rochester stood up and stretched. I grabbed my jacket and Rochester's leash and promised Lili that I'd be back soon to further demonstrate that happiness.

Ewan Stone's facility request arrived the next day, along with an email. "I know it's short notice, but the only time Professor Suleiman and the dog's handler can get up here is next week. Otherwise we'd have to wait until the fall."

I checked the calendar, and the following Monday afternoon was free, so I approved the requisition, and responded by email.

His answer came through quickly. "Great. I have two classes on Monday afternoon, and I'll bring them both."

He'd also attached an article about the effort to trace stolen artifacts from the Fertile Crescent, and I read through it. The area under investigation followed a vague quarter-moon shape, extending from the Nile River to the southern fringe of Turkey. It was bounded on the west by the Mediterranean Sea and on the east by the Persian Gulf.

The Tigris and Euphrates rivers flowed through the heart of the region, and I had studied in school that civilization was thought to have begun there, because the confluence of those rivers held unusually fertile soil, productive freshwater, and brackish wetlands. These produced an abundance of wild edible plant species.

Humans were able to experiment with the cultivation of grains and cereals and transition from hunter-gatherer groups to permanent agricultural societies. As such, it was a treasure trove of historical artifacts and one of the most archaeologically significant regions of the world.

With all the war in the region, people had been forced to illicit methods to feed their families, and many young men had turned to seeking out valuable items that could be shipped overseas.

Some had been excavated from tombs, while others were stolen from churches and mosques. They were usually small enough to fit into luggage, like pottery fragments, head statues, and bronze weapons.

I finally gave up my deep dive into the artifacts of the Fertile

Crescent, finished my other work, and opened the hacker laptop. I had only met Vic Davis once, when I accompanied him and his giant schnauzer, Schatzi, on one of his community surveys. He had seemed professional then—he had an iPad with a spreadsheet app, and he had an expensive-looking tool that resembled a camera which he used to take laser measurements of the trees.

Rochester was with me, and he had ignored Vic to sniff the female schnauzer. Once they had established a friendship, they both followed us as we walked the streets of my corner of River Bend.

I always tried to think the best of dog lovers, because I knew that dogs had a sixth sense about people that I had found trustworthy. But hey, if Vic had given Schatzi treats and belly rubs regularly, he could have been a lousy guy in all other respects.

I searched through property records for Vic Davis and Victor Davis, and found that he'd owned a home in south Jersey, which he had sold only a month before. He had also owned a home in Levittown, Pennsylvania, and that sale had closed only two days after the Jersey sale.

That combination was giving me a bad feeling. A guy sells two houses in short order, then announces that his business is closing and disappears. But I didn't know what else I could search for, legally.

I'd been able to hack into bank and phone records in the past. And if I downloaded the right software, and took a lot of risks, I could probably do it again. But I had promised Lili and my best friend, Rick Stemper, that I wouldn't do anything that might send me back to prison again.

Maybe Rick could help, though. As a police detective, he had access to information I couldn't get to legally. I texted him and asked if we could meet late that afternoon for coffee at the Chocolate Ear, in the center of Stewart's Crossing.

Rick and I had been acquaintances back in high school, when we'd been in a chemistry class together. When I returned home after prison I'd run into him at the Chocolate Ear, and we'd bonded over our divorces. Since then our lives had moved in parallel tracks—he'd met and married Tamsen Morgan and adopted her young son. I'd taken in Rochester and then met Lili.

He responded with 5:00 and a thumbs-up.

I put the phone down and looked at Rochester, who was staring up at me from his place on the floor. "What do you think, boy? What can Uncle Rick do to help us find Vic Davis?"

He rolled on his side and waved his front left paw in the air. I spoke dog enough to know that meant he wanted his tummy rubbed, so I sat beside him and obliged. While my hands were busy, my brain went into a meditative state. I liked Jennifer Dodge and thought she'd done a good job managing the tree committee. It wasn't her fault that Vic had skipped out, and she shouldn't take the blame for his bad actions.

I was going to help her to the best of my abilities. And in addition, I really didn't want to have to pay another assessment for tree removal, money that might otherwise go toward a wedding.

I imagined Rochester taking part in the ceremony, coming down the aisle with a box containing our wedding rings. How happy I would be to see him in that setting.

Then I remembered how delighted I had been to see Rochester after Lili and I spent a week in Florida in December. I hated to be away from my dog, though I knew other folks who happily boarded their dogs or sent them to doggy day care.

That reminded me of Vic's dog. "What happened to Schatzi?" I said out loud. "I could check with pet boarding places to see if he left her somewhere."

Rochester kicked me with his paw. "What? I'm not rubbing you enough? Are you still in a deficit from when we went away?"

He kicked me again.

"Duh. Of course. Rick could put out a missing persons alert on Vic. See if he took a flight anywhere."

I gave Rochester one more scratch under his chin and then jumped up. I used my office computer to search for pet boarding.

There were four places Vic could have left Schatzi in Levittown and I tried each one, using the same gambit. "My friend Vic left his giant schnauzer to board and he asked me to bring over a few of her favorite treats. But I lost the name of the place. Do you have Schatzi there?"

The answer in each case was no.

I put the phone down after the last call, frustrated. Rochester got up and nosed my leg again. "You are very needy," I said, as I stroked his head.

Rochester had gone through a lot before he came to me. A young couple with a baby had given him to a rescue group when they'd been overwhelmed between puppy and newborn. Then my next-door-neighbor, Caroline Kelly, had adopted him from the animal shelter a few months before she died.

"No," I said. "You don't think..."

Rochester looked up at me and woofed.

I called the Bucks County SPCA and asked if anyone had surrendered a black giant schnauzer recently. The clerk checked the records for me while I waited. "No record of a surrender in New Hope or Quakertown," she said.

I was relieved. Even though Vic was a jerk I didn't want to think he'd hand in his dog.

"But you could check with the Four Paws shelter in Yardley," she said. "Sometimes people drop dogs off with them."

I looked up the number, called, and asked about Schatzi. "Yes, she came in two days ago," the woman who answered said. "The owner said he was leaving the area and couldn't take her with him. Are you interested in adopting her?"

"Not right now," I said, and thanked her.

I looked at Rochester. "What a jerk, right, boy?"

He woofed in agreement.

Chapter 5

Temperature Rising

Rochester and I arrived at the Chocolate Ear at five. The café served great coffee and delicious pastries, and as a bonus, the owners had constructed an annex where humans and their canine companions could escape winter winds and summer heat.

It had a couple of other advantages. It was on the way to Friar Lake, and only a couple of blocks from Rick's office at the police station. And Gail Dukowski, who'd been my friend since she started the café, also baked special doggy biscuits which Rochester loved.

Though it was early spring, it was still too chilly to sit outside, so I settled him in the dog-friendly half of the café and walked over to the Dutch door to order coffee for me and a biscuit for him.

Gail's mother Lorraine came over to take my order. "You live in River Bend, don't you?" she asked after I told her what I wanted.

"I do."

"Everyone's been talking about the scandal over the tree removal," she said. "I never knew people to get so upset over a couple of trees."

Lorraine was a trim blonde in her fifties, her hair pulled behind her in a no-nonsense ponytail. "Are they upset about the removal, or about the company that was supposed to do the work?"

"Some of both," she said. "Two ladies were arguing this morning. One wants the trees gone, and the other doesn't. And then a third one said that the company that was supposed to remove them went bankrupt."

"The news is spreading," I said. I worried that Jennifer, and the rest of the members of the tree committee, would be in even more hot water as the whole community learned what had happened.

The coffees were ready as Rick arrived, and he took his from Lorraine. I gave Rochester a biscuit after he greeted Rick, and the three of us settled down at a table.

"What's new at the monk works?" Rick asked.

Rick and his stepson Justin watched a lot of documentaries, and one of them had been about a secret facility at Lockheed called the Skunk Works. Since then he'd taken to calling Friar Lake the monk works.

I told him quickly about the program we had upcoming. "Maybe Tamsen can bring Justin to see the demonstration," I said. "He'd probably like that."

"Text me the details," he said.

"I actually asked you here for some help with something at River Bend," I said. He already knew about the tree removal because I'd complained about it in the past. "Our contractor bailed on us, leaving us short a hundred grand. I did some quick research on him and it looks like he's done a runner."

I explained about the house sales and the office shutdown, and the way he'd dropped his dog off at the shelter.

"Really? He gave up his dog, too? What a jerk."

"Can you see if he left town on a plane?" I asked. "If he drove, he might have been able to take the dog with him."

"This isn't an official case," he said. "I don't have the authority to ask questions."

"He's a missing person."

"But no one has reported him to our office."

"I'm reporting him now," I said.

Rick picked up his coffee and sipped, then put it down. "Individuals over the age of 2 1 are adults and they have the right to choose to leave their established community without reporting that they are leaving."

"But he's a criminal!"

"That's a different story. What you're talking about is fraudulent business practice, which is investigated by the Commonwealth of Pennsylvania, not the Stewart's Crossing Police Department."

I frowned at him. "You're not helping."

"I'm trying to explain what to do. Someone from your HOA should report the crime to the state, and they'll investigate."

"But by then he could be thousands of miles away."

"He probably already is." He stared at me. "I know that look in your eyes. You've already been using your hacker laptop, haven't you?"

"Only legally," I said. "That's how I learned about the houses he sold. Jennifer Dodge heard about his bankruptcy from his office. And I called the animal shelters to see if he'd surrendered his dog."

"Great work. But I don't want you do anything that could get you into trouble." He sighed. "I have a little leeway because River Bend is under the jurisdiction of the SCPD. I'll make a few phone calls and see if I can find out what's going on with him."

I thanked him.

Rick and I finished our coffee, and I took Rochester home. Lili was waiting for us. "The rage about the trees is rising online," she said. "You need to look at Hi Neighbor. People are calling you names."

"Me? What have I done?"

"You're on the tree committee."

Lili had joined Hi Neighbor, an online community of IRL (in real life) neighbors, where they shared notices of lost cats and recommendations on plumbers and handymen. People posted information on crime and vandalism in neighboring areas as well.

Periodically, a topic would catch fire in the user groups of Hi Neighbor. A year before, we'd tried to remove the invasive ducks that had come to live around several of the lakes at the center of the community. I found them loud and was disgusted by the filth of their poop on the sidewalk, and I was happy when the association decided to get rid of them.

The company we hired pitched what they considered a humane way to relocate them, using baited traps. Several duck-loving neighbors had circulated petitions calling the crates "Duck-chau," which I thought was a reprehensible way of connecting the deaths of my distant relatives and other kin at the hands of the Nazis to moving a few web-footed pests somewhere else. I nearly lost my temper explaining that to one of the petition circulators, who called me a "Duck-hating dick!" and walked away.

Eventually the association had compromised. They made it against the rules to feed the ducks, and that lack of food caused many of the waterfowl to relocate voluntarily. They also asked the maintenance man to hose down the sidewalks to remove the duck poop, and we settled back into relative harmony.

Until the tree situation blossomed.

Vic had bailed on March 15. I should have known that the Ides of March would bring trouble. I was an English major and had read through most of Shakespeare's work between high school, college, and graduate school. But you always think that back-stabbing will happen to someone else.

I had no idea I would expose myself to the same level of vitriol by simply advocating for shade for myself and my dog as we walked around the community. Lili handed me her phone and I began to read the posts.

Several of them called out the members of the tree committee by name, with some curse words I wouldn't use for a right-wing politician or a mass murderer. "These people need to get a life," I said, as I pushed the phone back to Lili.

"You didn't get far enough," she said. "They're threatening to spray paint cars and throw rocks through windows."

"And if they do that, they'll get arrested, and see what it's like to have the weight of the law against them," I said, with only a bit of false bravado. In truth, I was more worried about what might happen to Rochester than to my car or our house. Suppose someone threw a rock at me, and hit him? I'd go ballistic. Nobody was going to hurt my furry child and get away with it.

Chapter 6

Bahamas Bound

My father, who was not a big holiday celebrator, said, "Everybody's Irish on St. Patrick's Day," and he always wore green that day and called himself "McNathan O'Levitan." He usually wore a dark green pullover sweater and a tie with shamrocks.

When I woke up the next day and realized it was March 17, I knew I had to carry on the family tradition, though I hated neckties. Instead I wore a pair of kelly green pants and a green and white striped Brooks Brothers shirt, both relics of my California years. I was glad I could still fit into them.

Lili was less a traditionalist than I was, though she did wear a green shamrock brooch she had bought while photographing the Troubles in northern Ireland. She was not a collector, as I was; every item in her wardrobe had a personal connection, from the butterfly hair clips she had bought from an artisan in Nicaragua to an embossed silver cup and saucer she had found in a souk in Beirut.

I was at Friar Lake working through emails when Rick called me. "I got a hit," he said. "Victor Davis boarded a flight from Philadelphia to Fort Lauderdale on Wednesday the 15th."

The Ides of March again. "Fort Lauderdale? Why would he head there?"

"No clue. But he didn't pick up a connecting flight, and he hasn't gotten one since then. He could be laying low in Florida, or he could be heading off to one of the islands. If he has a boat, he could be in the Bahamas by now."

"Don't we have an extradition treaty with them?"

"I don't know, Steve," Rick said, sounding exasperated. "We don't get many international criminals in Stewart's Crossing. Though I believe the only places we don't extradite are enemy nations like Cuba, North Korea and Iraq."

"So he could be headed for Cuba," I said. "Thanks for checking. I'll pass that on to the committee."

"I think you're jumping the gun with the Cuba idea. I'd hold that piece of information back if I were you."

"Will do." I put the phone down and looked outside, where I spotted a giant green shamrock moving slowly across the lawn. Rochester jumped up and put his paws on the windowsill, and he began barking.

Then I saw a pair of green legs under the shamrock, and remembered that we'd agreed the college's student life department could sponsor a party that afternoon. The shamrock-on-legs was one of the department's work-study students, and they were setting up their decorations.

I scratched behind Rochester's ears and told him it was okay, and then he and I went outside to see what was happening. Joey was already setting up long tables, and I helped Yelda Pasternak, the head of student life, put out the decorations.

"What are these?" I asked, holding up what looked like a black witch's cauldron carelessly sprayed with gold paint.

"We had them left over from Halloween," Yelda said. "Now they're leprechaun pots of gold. We'll fill them up with candy and give them out as prizes."

"You have an interesting name," I said. "Is it a version of Zelda?"

She shook her head. "It means girl in Hebrew."

"Oh, of course. I remember it being pronounced yel-DAH, though."

"My parents made an ill-fated attempt to move to Israel after they were married," she said. A cool breeze swept through Friar Lake, making the trees shake. "I was born there, and they argued over what my name should be. My father wanted a name from his side of the family, and my mother from her side. Neither of them would give, so the nurse wrote yel-DAH on my birth certificate. Girl."

She had five different bags of individual sized candy bars, and we began dividing them up into the cauldrons.

"My parents liked it so well they named my brother Yeled, which means boy."

I laughed. "Well, that takes the trouble out of baby names."

"We moved back to the US when I was three, and I got tired of telling people how my name was pronounced. Yelda was easier."

Around us, student workers were hanging long green streamers, positioning those giant shamrocks, and hanging green flags that read "Happy St. Patrick's Day."

I was glad that I'd worn green. One of the students tied a green bandana around Rochester's neck and then the kids all wanted to take pictures with him, which he graciously agreed to. While I watched my furry child, Yelda's comments about baby names brought up a memory.

As soon as Mary discovered she was pregnant, she and I had begun discussing baby names. Both her parents were still alive, as were mine, so we looked back a generation. She had a favorite great uncle named Bernard, so we considered B names in his memory. To appease my mother, to whom such things mattered, we promised we would consider her mother's name, Henrietta, for a girl, though we made it clear to her that Henrietta itself was off the table.

We ended up with Benjamin and Hannah —though of course we never needed either of those.

I shook those thoughts off as Yelda and I finished putting out the candy. Then I walked back to the student life van with her to retrieve some giant rainbows. The plan was to hide the pots behind the rainbows.

She grabbed the end of one rainbow. "We used these at Coming Out Day," she said. "I figured they'd work well today, too."

"I love the attitude," I said. "Reuse and repurpose."

"Our student workers are all interested in saving the planet," she said. "And they're eager to save trees by reusing paper products."

That reminded me of the tree project at River Bend. What were we going to do with all the trees that were removed? I supposed we could stack them at the clubhouse parking lot and offer them to homeowners to cut into logs. But not everyone in the neighborhood would be as good with a chain saw as Joey. Once we got a new contractor I'd have to ask Joey what he thought.

Rochester and I spent a happy couple of hours as buses from campus disgorged kids for the party and they romped around the property. The work-study students had special tags on their shirts identifying them as leprechauns, and if you recognized one you could "steal" his or her gold. That meant getting a raffle ticket for the candy-filled pots.

I really wanted a couple of tickets, but I had to remind myself that I was no longer a student. If I had to have a pot of candy, I could go to the grocery and buy one.

They finally began to clear out by four o'clock, and the work-study students and Joey's crew began to clean up.

I went into my office and pulled my hacker laptop out of my messenger bag. I'd been bringing it with me to Friar Lake since taking it down from the attic. It took a while to sort through boat registrations in Florida, but eventually I found that Vic owned a Bayliner 285D registered at the Lauderdale Marina on 15th Street. I called the dockmaster's office.

"I'm in trouble," I said to the woman who answered. "My flight to Fort Lauderdale was delayed and then cancelled and then rebooked, and I just landed at the airport." I tried to make my voice sound breathless. "I was supposed to take an Uber to your marina to meet my friend Vic for a trip to Nassau, and he's not answering his cell. I'm worried that he left without me."

"Do you know the name of the boat?" she asked.

"Arawn," I said, and I spelled it. I'd read my share of Welsh mythology as a teenager, so I knew that Arawn was the lord of the underworld. Fitting name for a thief's boat.

"You missed him by a day," she said, when she came back on the line. "He left on Thursday morning."

"Crap," I said. "All right, I'll try to get myself on a flight to Nassau and hook up with him there."

I looked at Rochester, who had been sitting at attention beside me as I spoke. The dog always seemed to know when I was stretching the truth—maybe it was something he smelled. I remembered those thousands of extra scent receptors he had. If an oncoming epileptic fit triggered a change in body chemistry, it wasn't a big jump to think that lying might do the same thing. Maybe someday we'll have canine lie detectors instead of mechanical ones.

"What do you think, boy? Has Vic Davis slipped away from us?"

He slumped down on the floor beside me. He'd demonstrated that he had some tracking ability during the winter, when we'd gone looking for a runaway teenager. But I guess once you get out of the country he couldn't help.

I emailed Jennifer and the rest of the committee. "Bad news. On Wednesday Davis flew to Fort Lauderdale, where he had a boat docked. He left Thursday morning, probably for the Bahamas."

It wasn't good news for River Bend. If Vic was gone and had liquidated his assets, then we wouldn't be able to recoup the hundred grand we'd already paid him.

Then I remembered the classic scene from the movie *Jerry Maguire*, when Cuba Gooding Jr., playing a high-priced athlete, kept repeating, "Show me the money!" to Tom Cruise, who portrayed his agent.

Where had our money gone? Could I find it?

My fingers hovered over the keyboard of the hacker laptop. In the past, with the right software, I'd been able to hack into a local bank. If Vic had his accounts there, I could update my tools and sneak in under the radar. If the money was still in a Tree-B-Gone account, I could set up a transfer to the HOA.

We'd have our money back and be able to hire another company to remove the trees. We'd still have a fight with the shade canopy folks, but Jennifer and I and the rest of the committee would be off the hook for losing a hundred grand.

Rochester jumped up and put his front paws on my thighs, sticking his big golden snout and black nose toward the keyboard.

It was enough to derail my train of thought. And then I realized all the problems with that idea. I might not have the right tools. Vic's bank might have solid security in place.

And if I was caught, I'd go to prison. Again.

With a snap, I closed the lid of the laptop and stuck my head down to Rochester's. "Thank you, boy," I said into his soft fur.

Chapter 7

Good Behavior

After dinner Friday night, while Lili was upstairs reading, I thought again about Vic Davis and his bank account. I knew I couldn't do anything illegal, but I wondered if he'd been as quick to close out his account as he had been to shut down his office. If I could find out where he banked, the HOA's attorneys could approach the bank and try to get his account frozen.

I sat at the dining room table with the hacker laptop open, and Rochester came over and curled up against my leg, a constant pressure that reminded me to stay on the right side of the law. It took a while, but eventually I found a complaint online by an angry customer of Vic Davis's. "He was pretty quick to deposit my check in his account at Quaker State Bank," she wrote. "I wish he'd been as quick to remove the tree from my yard."

Soon after I returned to Stewart's Crossing, I'd had cause to investigate that bank, and discovered how ineffective their online security was. My fingers tingled as I remembered how I had been able to use sniffers to find an open port on an employee computer connected to the bank's network.

From there, I was able to gather the information I needed. At the time, I was trying to understand how money in the account of an old friend of my parents' had been stolen. I hadn't used anything I learned for my own profit, just to help Edith Passis.

But I knew that any attempt to get into their computer systems might trigger an investigation that could ultimately lead to me. It was frustrating, but I accepted that I couldn't even verify that Tree-B-Gone's account was still active without getting myself into much more trouble.

I tried every legal means I could think of, but I couldn't find evidence that Vic had accounts anywhere else. I didn't know if that was good or bad. Sometimes criminals will spread their business among several different banks. In Vic's case, if he knew that he was going to steal money from clients, he might have set up accounts at multiple local banks, manipulating their policies for approving deposits. Before leaving, for example, he might have been able to withdraw some percentage more cash than he actually had in the bank.

One scam I'd learned about involved putting dollar-sized pieces of paper into a night deposit or an ATM, telling the machine you were depositing, say, a thousand dollars in cash. Then you could use the same ATM to withdraw a grand. Some ATMs were still not sophisticated enough to realize you'd made a junk deposit, though I'd read that machines were going to be able to photograph a deposit and verify the bills.

I was determined to find out where Vic had stashed that hundred grand. To determine the legitimacy of the deposit, as well as to thwart potential fraud and prevent potential losses from risky deposits, a bank could take as long as nine business days to clear a hundred-thousand-dollar check like the one from River Bend. If Vic's account was new, they might only give him immediate access to the first $5,000 of a check and make him wait for the rest.

But if he was playing a longer game and defrauding multiple homeowners' associations, he might set up different accounts, and then run small transactions through them to become a valued client.

Then he'd be able to skip the waiting period and get full access to the money.

If he was doing that, he'd have to have multiple accounts. Why couldn't I find them? It was frustrating and I felt more and more temptation to hack.

Rochester came over to me then, sniffing my knee and smiling up at me. He was the angel on my shoulder, keeping me out of trouble. I turned off the laptop and moved over to the living room, where I picked up the mystery novel I was reading on my Kindle. That shifted my attention, and by the time I took Rochester for his late walk, I was at peace with my decision not to try hacking into the bank. Vic Davis was the criminal here, and I wasn't going to let him or anyone else provoke me into criminal acts.

Saturday morning I was walking Rochester when Malgorzata Stopnicki, the white-haired lady who had threatened me with her cane, cut through between two blocks of townhouses, and her Westie began barking like mad.

Rochester thinks that every dog who barks at him wants to play, and I often have to wrestle him away. I was trying to control him when the woman started talking to me. The dog's barking was so loud that I couldn't make out what she was saying, but I could tell she was angry.

"Lady, I can't hear you if your dog keeps barking," I said.

"Don't call me lady like some stranger!"

"Okay, then, you don't want to be lady I'll call you sir. I've gotta go." I turned on my heel and started dragging Rochester, who didn't want to follow me. Sometimes you're the dog, and sometimes you're the sled. I did the pulling for the first fifty feet, then he romped ahead and I had to put the brakes on or I'd have gone tumbling.

"What was that about, boy?" I asked. Usually our neighbors were very polite, even the ones with barking dogs. The Westie was still yapping when we were half a block away, and I heard another dog join the cacophony. I felt sorry for any neighbor who was trying to sleep in.

I turned a corner with Rochester and came right up against Pete Szabo on his three-wheeled bicycle. Fortunately my dog and I were both on the grass so we avoided a collision. "Any news on our lost landscaper?" he asked. "Is he coming back?"

"I don't think so. He sold his house and left his dog with a rescue. Then he flew to Fort Lauderdale and picked up a boat he had there. The marina thinks he went to the Bahamas, but no one is sure."

"How did you find out all that?"

"A bit of research," I said. "And some help from the police."

"Doesn't sound like a legal kind of research," he said. "Or something the police would tell you."

My pulse began to race and I stared at him. "Are you accusing me of doing something illegal? Because I've had it with people making out like this is all the fault of the committee. We're volunteers and neighbors and I don't appreciate the kind of language I've been seeing on Hi Neighbor."

"I don't trust anybody on the board, or any of your committees, either," he said. "You're all out for yourselves."

"And you're an idiot." I tugged Rochester's leash and moved forward.

"I've got my eye on all of you!" he called behind me.

I was very unsettled by the time we got home. I had always considered my walks with Rochester a special time between us, when we could be out in nature and relish our connection. I didn't want to be afraid to go out my door because someone might yell at me.

Lili had invited Joey and Mark for dinner that evening, so she wanted to head to the farmer's market and see what was fresh. I went with her, even though it meant I had to leave Rochester at home. I was sure that he understood my unhappiness about the confrontations, and I didn't want to keep spreading my unease to him.

Lili was happy to find some big eggplants at the market, and we decided on eggplant parmigiana, along with a salad of baby lettuce and some garlic bread. We bought what we could there and then stopped at the grocery for the rest.

We were about to head to the checkout line when I ran into Jennifer Dodge. "You're one of the few neighbors I'm not frightened to see," she said. "Have you been getting harassment from people?"

Lili moved into the line while I stood with Jennifer and told her about the two who'd approached me that morning. "And it looks bad on Hi Neighbor, too," I said.

She nodded. "Two different people have accused me of being in cahoots with Vic Davis," she said. "One of them asked me how much he paid me to give him the contract."

"That's really obnoxious," I said. "I tried to tell this one man that we're all volunteers and neighbors, and that it wasn't our fault he ran off with the money, but he ended up threatening me."

She rubbed her upper shoulders with her hands. "The whole thing makes me want to run away for a while." She laughed. "Maybe the Bahamas. That would get the rumor mill going, wouldn't it?"

I laughed and told her I hoped that as time went on the furor would die down.

Lili and I returned home and began working together to cook dinner. As I peeled and sliced the eggplant for her, she asked, "What were you looking for last night?"

So she knew I'd been on the hacker laptop.

"I wanted to see if I could figure out where Tree-B-Gone banked," I said. "I found a customer who mentioned Vic used Quaker State Bank, but I didn't break into the bank and check his account."

"Could you have, if you wanted to?"

"Two years ago, I probably could have," I said. "My skills were sharper then, and security procedures were a lot laxer. Today, I'd have to be really committed to do something like that."

"Define really committed."

I began handing her the eggplant slices so she could dip them in egg and flour. "You've met Edith Passis," I said. "My old piano teacher."

"Yes. She seems very sweet."

"She is. And some creeps took advantage of her and I hacked into the bank to figure out what was going on."

She began sautéing the eggplant slices as I prepared two rectangular baking pans for her.

"You didn't get caught," she said.

"I didn't. I was careful, and like I said, security was lot laxer back then." I began pouring tomato sauce into two large pans. "I've never used my hacking skills to steal anything or hurt anyone."

"I know. Which is why I don't complain when I see that machine on the table."

The sauté pan began sizzling, and Lili flipped the eggplant slices. "But I like to be reassured now and then," she said.

"You can be reassured," I said. "And besides, you have Rochester on your side. He never lets me get into trouble."

She laughed. "I'm not sure I believe that. Half the time it's Rochester getting you into trouble."

We worked together to finish the dish, layering eggplant, cheese, mushrooms and sauce, and then she slid both pans into the oven.

"We have some time before Joey and Mark get here," she said. "Would you like to be rewarded for your good behavior?"

I smiled and kissed her. "I would like nothing better."

Rochester began to bark, and Lili and I had to lock him out of the bedroom.

Chapter 8

Joining Together

A couple of years before, Joey had adopted an English cream golden retriever, a white ball of fluff and enthusiasm he called Brody. He and Rochester tore up the house whenever they were together, and that evening wasn't any different. As soon as Joey and Mark arrived, Brody pushed past them into our house and took off with Rochester.

While Rochester was certainly spoiled, he obeyed basic commands—except when Brody was around, because Brody got away with murder from Mark and Joey. So Rochester felt he was entitled to go wild, racing up and down the stairs, barking his fool head off, and charging up to whichever human was closest.

"I'm sorry," Mark said. "He's really much better at home." He grabbed the white golden's collar and dragged him over to the couch. Mark was very, very tall and he was able to use his long legs to corral the dog. Joey brought him a glass of white wine and sat beside him.

"This tree business is getting out of hand," Joey said, when Rochester settled on the floor and Lili and I sat across from the boys with our own glasses of wine. "This morning I was up on a ladder trimming the oak in front of our house and this white-haired old lady

47

mistook me for somebody replacing the arborist that stole the money."

He shook his head. "If my mother heard the language she used, she would have slapped that woman silly. But I was trained to respect my elders, even if they're as nutty as fruitcakes."

"Did she have a white Westie with her?" I asked.

"You know her?"

"She's been after me," I said. "She almost hit me with her cane at the board of directors meeting."

"And I thought River Bend was going to be such a pleasant place to live," Mark said. He looked at Joey. "You told me River Bend would be perfect for us. Quiet, nice neighbors and beautiful land-scaping."

Joey grinned sheepishly and then squeezed Mark's hand. "It will be."

"It usually is," I added. "But it's something about this tree busi-ness that's turning neighbor against neighbor."

I met Mark when I returned home to Stewart's Crossing. He ran an antique shop in the center of town and we were both part of a book group for a few months. Then when I began work at Friar Lake and met Joey, I decided to introduce them.

I know, it was silly to think that because they were both gay and tall, that they'd get along, but they did. After a while Joey and Brody had moved into the apartment over the antique shop where Mark lived, and then a year later Joey and Mark had bought a townhouse a few blocks from us.

The dogs were quiet enough by then that we thought it was safe to start eating dinner. But both of them kept moving between our legs and under the table, waiting for a handout or some dropped food. "There is nothing here for you, Bro," Joey said. "You won't eat eggplant and you can't have garlic bread."

Brody clearly didn't listen, though eventually Rochester settled in the corner, right in my sight line, with a baleful look on his face. Finally I got up and gave them both peanut-butter biscuits.

After dinner Joey and I took the dogs for a walk, and Lili and Mark handled the clean up together. I was pleased that they got along so well. When you date someone, or marry them, you have to incorporate them into your friend group, and then extend that to the significant others of your friends, too. I'd been lucky that Lili was happy with everyone, from Rick and Tamsen to Joey and Mark to Tor and his wife Sherri, who lived in New York.

At Christmas, Lili and I spent a lot of time with her brother Fedi and his wife Sara and their kids, and I met a bunch of Lili's other cousins, who were all boisterous Jews with Cuban or Latin American heritage. I felt a bit overwhelmed sometimes by their rapid speech and their effusive hugs and kisses, but I was getting better around them. I also had met a bunch of friends Lili had made during her years as a freelance photojournalist, including one who wrote for the *Wall Street Journal* and another who ran her favorite restaurant in Brooklyn.

Fortunately the only people who passed Joey and me that evening while we walked were in cars, so we didn't have to worry about getting harassed again. But I resolved to get up extra early on Sunday morning to walk Rochester before many others were out.

The combination of good friends, good wine and rich desserts defeated that idea, and I slept long after I should have. Rochester had been tired out by Brody, so he let me sleep.

My delayed start time meant that most of the people we usually saw when walking had already gone back inside. But I still felt nervous each time we rounded a corner.

My fear of running into people I knew led me to wonder about Vic's friends. Did he have any? Perhaps a friend in the Bahamas? By the time we got home I was eager to do another deep dive into Vic Davis, this time focused on social media. Lili had gone out to take some photos, so I was on my own.

I used the hacker laptop, with the additional safeguard of incognito windows. Once again, Rochester curled against my leg.

I started with Facebook, where Vic had about fifty friends. I copied their names into an Excel spreadsheet. Then I began reviewing the photos he had posted. There weren't very many, and most of them related to the previous business he had run, such as photos of the items he had bought for resale.

He had purchased a whole pallet of colored lights meant to be installed in your toilet bowl, so you could find it without turning on a light and disturbing someone sleeping. Sets of individual silicone lemon squeezers and ice cube trays in the shape of the United States. Water bottles shaped like hand grenades. Blankets in the shape of giant tortillas. No wonder he had been able to buy them in bulk, heavily discounted.

In a few cases he'd posted "Anyone know what this is?" A picture of a pair of silicone and metal forks had been identified as back-scratchers. An odd-shaped brush was something to scrape your razor blades clean with.

I did find one photo of his boat, the Arawn, on the stern. Beneath it was the "hailing port," which was listed as Bimini, BS. That was a good clue, because I thought the hailing port was the place where your boat was registered.

Unfortunately, I discovered the hailing port could be anywhere you chose—even a landlocked location. If you were sailing your boat around the world, you might use your hometown as a way of generating conversation with other yachties.

But it did mean that Vic had a connection to Bimini. During Prohibition, it was a favorite hangout for rumrunners, because it was so close to the Florida coast. I started going through all his friends, looking at who they were and trying to figure out how they were connected to him. I spotted Vic in a group of deep-sea fishermen, and in a reunion of his high school pals. But nothing more than that.

Finally I gave up. But one of the photos I saw spiked a memory of my own. A Jewish boy at his bris, the ritual circumcisions Jewish boys go through at eight days old. The baby rested on an ornate silver tray, of the kind my mother put pastries on at formal events. Silver dollars had been arrayed in a circle around the baby. Adoring relatives stood in the background. I imagined there had been a similar photo taken of me at my bris.

Lili came in then, carrying her camera in one gloved hand and using the other to undo a scarf around her neck. "It's chilly out there," she said. "But the sky is an amazing blue. I drove up Ferry Street into the country searching for barns, and I got some terrific shots."

I stood up and kissed her cold cheek, and took her coat. "That's great."

"What have you been up to?" she asked, as she looked down at the photo on my computer screen.

"Thinking about my bris," I said. "Not that I remember any of it, but I got curious. See all those coins around the baby?"

I slid into my chair and she sat beside me. "The coins represent a tradition called the pidyon ha-ben, or redemption of the son. Parents can only do it if they have a first-born son. Because you're older than Fedi is, it wouldn't have applied to him."

"The way that photo is framed it looks like the baby is about to be eaten," she said.

"The way my mother had described it to me, my parents' relatives and friends each gifted a silver dollar, which were laid out around me like that. Then the mohel lifts the baby up to do the circumcision."

I sat back. "My father used to joke, 'You know why you don't pay a mohel? He takes tips!'"

I could hear him in my head, repeating that joke, and I laughed, as Lili did too.

"So then, after completing the circumcision, the mohel turns to the parents and asks, in all seriousness, if they want to keep the baby, or take the money. The correct answer, of course, is the baby, and the money is gathered up and put aside for the child's future."

"Do you still have those coins?" Lili asked.

"I saw them once or twice when I was growing up. My father promised to hand them over to me when I had my first son." I shrugged. "Well, he must have figured out that wasn't going to happen. I vaguely remember a box in the attic labeled "Steve" that I glanced at when I moved in. Maybe the silver dollars are there."

Lili stood up. "Well, if you find them, let me know. We could put them in a presentation box or something."

She went into the kitchen and I looked back at the photo of some stranger's bris. I wasn't going to spend the silver dollars, but I thought it would be nice to have them close, as a memory of my parents and the traditions they had established for me.

Before I climbed up in the attic to look for the box, I searched online for the meaning of the tradition. I discovered that my mother had been confused.

Instead of asking the parents to choose between the baby and the money, the father was supposed to put the baby on a silver platter and offer him to a kohen, a descendant of the first priest, Aaron. It was a symbolic way of returning his first-born son to God.

Then the kohen was supposed to accept the coins, originally five shekels, in place of the child. The ceremony was to remind us of the way that God had taken all the first-born sons of Egypt when Moses demanded the freedom of his people. Those sons belonged to God, so this was a symbolic way of referencing that event.

Interesting. I was always fascinated by the way things my mother or father told me had been warped by time, memory, or their faulty knowledge of Yiddish, which is how they would have heard those stories in the first place.

My mother came from a close-knit family in Trenton, and I was the first boy in my generation, so I was sure that my bris and pidyon ha-ben had been big events. It was time for me to reclaim that part of my heritage.

This time Rochester didn't bother to follow me out to the garage to get the ladder. That might have been because Lili had given him a cookie in the kitchen.

I climbed the stairs to the second floor, taking care not to bang the ladder against the wall, and set it up under the ceiling hatch. But I had to climb up so that my head was above the ceiling in order to look around. I pulled the long cord that switched on the single light bulb.

We tried not to keep much stuff in the attic. Lili was very opposed to keeping stuff unless it had meaning to her, so everything up there belonged to me or my parents. I moved a couple of boxes around until I found the one with my name on it.

"Do you need help?" Lili called from downstairs.

"Yeah. Can I hand this box down to you?"

"I'll be right there." In a moment she was climbing the stairs, and I lifted the box up and carefully descended a couple of rungs until I could hand it safely to her. She carried it into our bedroom and I followed once I had turned off the light and closed the hatch.

Rochester was already in the bedroom with her. By the time I got there, she had wiped a layer of dust off the top of the box and laid it on a bathroom towel over the bedspread.

I began lifting things out. The first thing on top was a folded piece of linen that I recognized. I unfolded it carefully, and then, quite unexpectedly, began to cry.

"What's the matter?" Lili asked. She put her hand on my shoulder.

"I feel like something's been stolen from me," I said, when I was able to speak again. "Do you know what a wimpel is?"

"The thing that the flying nun wore that let her take off?"

I laughed. "Different spelling. This is w-i-m-p-e-l."

I sat there with the linen on my lap. "When I was born, my great-uncle had a friend who was a German immigrant, Mrs. Altman. She told him about this tradition that German Jews had. You take the cloth that wraps the baby boy at his bris and then you decorate it with his Hebrew name and some symbols."

I held the cloth up to her. "This is my Hebrew name, Shmuel Chaim. The shofar represents my first name, which translates as to 'called by God.' And the two wine glasses toasting each other represent 'to life.'"

"Your family was very religious."

"My grandparents were. And I was the first male grandchild, so they went all out, including the pidyon ha-ben I told you about."

I started to sniffle again. "Mary and I never even learned the sex of the babies we lost. They could have been boys."

"Would you have used that wimpel for them?"

I shook my head. "No, it's mine. When I had my bar mitzvah, we dug it out and used it to wrap the Torah I read from. And then we were supposed to use it to wrap the Torah at an aufruf before my wedding to Mary. But by then it was lost."

I shrugged. "But we did every other Jewish thing possible, down to my breaking the glass." I smiled. "I smashed it the first time. Though that was supposed to be a good omen for the marriage, things didn't work out that way."

She took my hand. "When we get married, we'll both smash glasses. Give us double the good luck."

I squeezed her hand. "Any further thoughts on that wedding?"

"I want to invite Fedi and Sara and their kids, and I wouldn't ask them to come up here from Florida in the winter. But I'd also like to do something outdoors, and so that lets out high summer. Maybe early fall? Foliage could be a nice backdrop. And we could do it at Columbus Day weekend to make it easier for people who are traveling."

"Or Indigenous People's Day, if you're so inclined," I said, smiling. "I thought you wanted to be married in a synagogue, since you didn't get to do that the first two times."

"Do you think we could have a ceremony at Shomrei Torah? And then maybe the reception at Friar Lake?"

"I forgot to renew my membership at Shomrei Torah after the rabbi's brother died," I said. "Going there got to be creepy for me. I kept remembering his body on the grass outside the sanctuary."

"A different synagogue, then?" Lili asked.

"No, I'll get over it. Shomrei Torah for the service, Friar Lake for the reception. Should we ask Rabbi Goldberg to officiate? I haven't spoken to him since I stopped going to the Torah study sessions."

"If you'd like. But I'd like to meet him first."

"I'm sure that rabbis require you to come in before the ceremony," I said.

"That's another thing we'll have to add to our calendar," Lili said. She pulled out her phone. "I downloaded this wedding planning app. You can select from a bunch of different appointment choices, like having a gown fitting or a cake testing, or put in your own."

As she typed, I was grateful that such an app hadn't existed when Mary and I got married. Instead she'd carried around a three-ring binder with photos and recipes and sample text for the ketubah, the marriage contract, in both Hebrew and English. I could only imagine what else she'd have added if she had an app to prompt her.

"Here it is," Lili said. "Meeting with officiant. This app is so great —I can send you the task to set up the meeting, and then once you set it up, it will send the appointment to my calendar."

It was clear that I was going to be much more involved in planning this wedding than I had been in my ceremony with Mary. That had to be a good thing.

"When are you thinking of announcing our engagement?"

"We should give people plenty of notice before the wedding. The app suggests sending out "save the date" announcements as soon as you have it." She looked back down at her phone. "There are a bunch of samples here I can send to you for your review."

"You're making this sound like a business project."

"Well, it is a big deal." She looked over at me. "Or don't you think so?"

I reached out and took her hand. "Committing my life to you is certainly a big deal," I said. "I don't want the planning to overwhelm what this means to us. The most important thing is that I love you and you love me..."

Before I could finish, she repeated the sing-song words from Barney the Dinosaur. "And we're a happy family."

I laughed, and Rochester stuck his nose between us to join in the fun.

I looked at her. "So we're doing the whole thing? Printed invitations with reply cards? A synagogue service with Fedi giving you away in a white gown?"

"I think I'm beyond the white gown," Lili said. "But yeah, I'd like the rest of it. And a cake. Definitely a cake."

I squeezed her hand again. "I can certainly get behind a cake."

"We have to get moving," Lili said. "Let's plan to send out the save the date cards in the next two weeks. Then we have to send out the actual invitations four to five months before the date we choose."

I counted backwards. "So that means we send out the invitations sometime in May?"

She nodded. "And it will take a while to get them printed."

I could see a cash register somewhere in the background going ka-ching, ka-ching, but it didn't matter. Lili and I were getting married and I wanted the ceremony and the reception to be everything she dreamed of.

I carefully folded the wimpel and put it aside. After some more poking around in the box, I found a ragged plastic bag with the silver dollars inside. I opened it and spilled them into my hands. "The last hands to touch these were probably my father or mother," I said.

I looked over at Lili. "And they represent the fact that so many people cared about me from the time I was born. Gives you something to live up to, doesn't it?"

"I think your parents, and all those people who brought silver dollars, would be proud of the man you've become," Lili said.

"Not so proud of the divorce, the conviction or the prison time."

"You can't separate out any one part of your life. It all works together to make you who you are. I'm not particularly proud of my two failed marriages, but I'm willing to try again. With you."

Chapter 9

Pottery Sherds

T he chill over the weekend had caused some of the trees at Friar Lake to drop their buds, and then the wind had made a mess of the place, tossing over trash cans and decorative signs, so Joey and his crew had to focus on cleanup on Monday morning while I did paperwork. I did take Rochester out for a run in the middle of the morning, as I checked over the places where we planned to host Professor Edwin Suleiman and the dog who'd been trained to hunt for ancient artifacts.

The professor arrived at one o'clock for the two o'clock demo. He was accompanied by Blake Crisp, the handler from the Working Dog Center at the University of Pennsylvania, and his yellow lab, Archie.

Suleiman was a distinguished-looking gent in his early sixties, in a green loden-cloth jacket with leather elbow patches. While I was showing them the property, he lit up a pipe with aromatic tobacco that smelled like cherries.

Blake was much younger, probably barely thirty. He kept Archie on a tight leash and the dog didn't seem to mind, happy to stay close to his handler. I wondered if Archie was a Velcro dog like Rochester, and what in his past might have caused him to behave that way. Was it all training?

"How did you pair up with Archie?" I asked, as we walked around.

"We have a couple of breeders we work with who look at the puppies they raise for the qualities we want. We need dogs with a strong drive—a willingness, enthusiasm or vigor to engage in the kind of behaviors we want. I met Archie when he was about six weeks old, and he was already demonstrating that he loved to play."

I looked at the way Rochester was interacting with the yellow lab. While my dog went down on his front paws in an invitation to play, Archie kept his head up and remained by Blake's side.

"Really? He doesn't look that playful."

"I've been working with him for over a year," Blake said. "He's been trained to know that he has to complete a task before he's released to play. Right now he's obeying the cues I'm giving him, that we're here to work."

Perhaps that's why Rochester didn't like Archie. The yellow lab was all business, while Rochester wanted to play. When he couldn't convince Archie to join in, he turned to Professor Suleiman, jumping up on him.

"Rochester, stop that!" I said. My golden was accustomed to being the center of attention, and I was embarrassed by his behavior. He finally calmed down when Suleiman scratched behind his ears.

"Your dog clearly has a strong drive for affection," Blake said. "If he was younger, I'm sure he could be trained to focus that drive, whether it's search and rescue, identifying explosives, sniffing out narcotics, helping diabetics control their health, or cancer detection."

That made me feel better about Rochester, even though I wanted him to make me proud and show some discipline.

"We're what we call a foundation program," Blake continued. "We teach the basic skills necessary for a successful career in detection. We like to think of it as a liberal arts degree that will prepare them to go on to the advanced training that best suits their physical and behavioral strengths."

He looked down at Archie. "He's getting some advanced training now, based on my work with Dr. Suleiman. But that doesn't mean he'll continue in this area. He could get additional training for explosives, drugs or medical detection before he's permanently placed."

We continued toward the chapel. "How many people are you expecting this afternoon?" Suleiman asked.

"Professor Stone is bringing two classes, which should be about forty students," I said. "Yelda Pasternak from student life is bringing a van full too. I thought we could use the chapel for the presentation. There are a lot of good hiding places there."

We walked all around the property just in case, and Blake decided that the former chapel was the best place to hide things for Archie to find.

"Rochester would agree with your decision," I said, reaching down to scratch his head. "He's always hiding his toys and chew bones somewhere and I end up on the floor retrieving them."

He twisted his head around to lick my hand.

Suleiman had brought two artifacts with him from the museum at Penn. Well, they weren't artifacts so much as remnants of artifacts. Professor Suleiman, who told me to call him Ed, apologized and said he couldn't take anything valuable out of the collection for these demos, so he had picked on a couple of large fragments.

"We call these pottery sherds, and they're some of the most useful 'fossils' the prehistorian can deal with," Ed said. "Because cooks have been breaking pots and dishes since the beginning of time, pottery is particularly useful for correlating in time various cultural levels from different regions."

"I noticed you used the word sherd rather than shard," I said. "What's the difference?"

"A 'sherd' is a broken piece of pottery with sharp edges, and we usually use it for items that have been found on an archaeological site. The words shard and sherd are interchangeable, though archaeologists prefer sherd because it's more specific."

He held up one buff-colored piece. "This comes from the rim of a large water jar," he said. The other piece was a darker color, and he said that it was the handle of a similar jar.

When Eastern bought the abbey property from the monks who had owned it, we restored and renovated the buildings, while trying to retain their character. So while we'd taken away the religious iconography, there was still a raised wooden dais at the far end of the nave, with low doors that led to storage areas we didn't use. The curved wall was lined with niches that held statues of saints.

Ed had brought a laptop with him for the presentation, and he and I set it up on the dais while Rochester romped around the chapel and Archie sat sedately by the front door.

With Archie focused outside, Blake looked around for the best hiding spots. When we had the PowerPoint geared up and ready to go, Blake asked us to take Archie away so there was no way that the dog could see where he put the items. Ed took Archie's leash and I took Rochester and we went outside.

Rochester peed—probably to remind Archie that this was his property. Archie looked supremely nonchalant. Ewan Stone arrived in his SUV with a group of his students, and others followed in their own cars and trucks, trailing up the hill in a small caravan. At the far end I saw the college van.

Ewan shook Ed's hand effusively. "Thanks so much for coming up here," he said.

"It's a beautiful spot. Is this what the rest of your campus looks like?" Ed asked.

"It's all Collegiate Gothic," Ewan said. "There wasn't any original connection between the college and this property, which was called Our Lady of the Waters, until Eastern bought it a couple of years ago to renovate. But you're right, the architecture is very similar."

Rick's wife Tamsen arrived then with Justin, who looked

delighted to have gotten out of school early. I hoped the presentation wouldn't be too boring for him. I went over to greet them with Rochester, and Justin got down on his knees and buried his head in the golden's side.

"Not a good day at school," Tamsen whispered to me. "I'm glad I could take him out early."

Rochester turned his neck to sniff Justin's hair, and then licked him once. Justin pulled away, laughing, and the four of us walked into the back of the chapel. I sent Tamsen and Justin up front but stayed in the back with Rochester to direct any latecomers.

Ewan Stone stepped up onto the dais and introduced Blake and Archie, and Professor Suleiman, who brought up his first screen, the logos of the organizations behind the presentation.

"Working dogs like Archie are vital assets in helping detect hidden narcotics, explosive devices, and other illicit products," Ed said. "Now the Working Dog Center at the University of Pennsylvania School of Veterinary Medicine and the Penn Museum are part of an effort to see if dogs' keen ability to identify and distinguish odors may assist in the effort to prevent smuggling of archaeological artifacts."

He flipped to another screen of a dog sniffing luggage at the airport. "Just as a narcotics detection dog can make a drug search that much easier, we're hoping that these dogs may be able to help law enforcement officials identify antiquities that have been illegally collected."

I moved up to the front of the chapel with Rochester so that I could switch the lights on when the presentation was over. I noticed Rochester was watching the presentation intently, the way sometimes he sat beside Lili and me and focused on the television—especially if there was a dog on the program.

The next slide was a map of the Fertile Crescent. "This area, often called the cradle of civilization, has also been in contention between various groups for centuries. Using scents derived from legally collected artifacts currently in the Penn Museum's collection,

Blake is training four dogs to identify the scents of archaeological objects from regions where terrorist groups are profiting from the looting of antiquities."

While I was fascinated, Rochester clearly wasn't. He went down on his belly and began sniffing along the bottom of the dais.

Ed flipped to another slide. "Ancient objects like coins or cylinder seals, looted from archaeological sites, are small enough to be concealed in a pocket, making them a low-risk prospect for smugglers, who profit from a high mark-up after the artifacts enter illegal markets in places like the U.S., Germany, and Japan. Deploying dogs like Archie will help us intercept those smugglers."

His last screen showed a group of dogs in training. I was surprised to see a basset hound along with a German shepherd and two labs, one of which I thought was Archie. I noticed that Rochester had scooted away from me, still along the bottom of the dais, to the point where he was right beneath Ed's podium.

Ed nodded to me, and I turned on the lights. He shut down the projector and stepped out from behind the table to face the audience. "And now, what you really want is to see Archie in action, am I right?"

The audience applauded. In the front row, Justin leaned forward.

Blake knelt beside Archie and unhooked his leash. "Find," he said, and the lab took off, nose down. Rochester looked up at the dais.

I had to hold Rochester back because he wanted to get in on the action. And he did have some experience at search and rescue—a few months before he'd helped Rick and me find a criminal who'd gotten lost in the snow.

We all watched as Archie sniffed around the statues in niches behind the dais, then gave up and jumped down to the stone floor and joined Rochester on the floor, sniffing the wooden doors that led to the crawl space beneath the dais. Ed came down the other side to stand beside me.

I didn't know where Blake had hidden the sherds so I was

watching Archie as eagerly as the rest of the crowd. I hoped that Rochester wasn't getting in his way.

There were four doors into the crawl space under the dais, and Archie and Rochester were both fascinated by one of them in particular. Archie sniffed for a moment, then sat on his haunches and gave one sharp bark.

"That's his signal," Blake said. He pursed his lips and cocked his head. "Let's see what he's found."

He came down the steps and over to the door, and both dogs backed away. He leaned down and grabbed a wooden knob, which he tugged forward. I realized that I'd never looked under there and wondered what else was there.

Archie went down on all fours and barked one more time as Ed pulled out a plastic storage bin. Rochester barked along with him, and looked over to me, a big doggy grin on his face.

"That's funny," Ed said to me. "Blake doesn't usually use plastic bins as hiding places. He says the plastic smell can interfere with the dog's nose."

Even if the sherds weren't in the box, Blake was playing along with the dog. Maybe this was part of the demo, that the dog found the wrong thing first, then the right one.

Blake knelt down and removed the lid from the plastic bin, and then lifted out a small wooden box. He looked as confused as I felt as he opened it. He pulled out a string of beads and then examined a tag at the end of the string. "Professor Suleiman? Could you come over here and take a look at what Archie has found?"

Ed hurried over there and took the string from Blake. "These appear to be lapis lazuli and blue glass beads with gold ornaments interspersed and a gold pendant," he said. He looked at Blake. "Did you put these here?"

Blake shook his head.

Chapter 10

Unexpected Results

"That's not what I put out for Archie," Blake said. "Can we put that container aside and let Archie search again?"

"Certainly." Ed nodded to me, and I walked over to the bin, replaced the cover, and tried to lift it. It was heavy, and Ed took one side of it. We carried it over to the side of the chapel. Rochester followed us, sniffing at the bin, but Archie remained back by the dais.

"Okay," Blake said brightly. "Let's try this again. Normally I'd give Archie a reward after a successful search, but this wasn't what he was supposed to find."

He knelt beside Archie again and repeated the Find command. But Archie didn't go much further, just to the next door under the dais.

Rochester rushed back to join Archie at the dais. He sat on his hind legs and barked, as he'd seen Archie do. A moment later, Archie did the same thing.

From Blake's body language I could tell the artifact wasn't behind that door either, but he went through with the procedure. Sure enough, there was another plastic bin behind door number two. Blake looked inside it, and produced a treat from his pocket. "Good boy," he said to Archie.

Rochester looked up at him, and Blake laughed. "You deserve a treat, too, Rochester," he said, and he gave my dog a tiny cookie in the shape of a bone.

Then he climbed up onto the dais and walked over to one of the statues, which I hadn't realized was loose, and pulled forward on it. One sherd was hidden there, and he held it up. "This is what I hoped Archie would find. But remember, this is still an experimental program, and Archie would get a lot more scent-specific training if we decide it's worthwhile to deploy him in this capacity."

He then walked across to the other side of the chapel. "As Professor Suleiman has said, because of their keen ability to discern different scents, dogs can serve in many different roles. At the Working Dog Center all dogs go through basic scent training, and then we decide, based on their abilities, which area they will specialize in. Archie may end up helping a child with epilepsy learn to control her seizures, or as a cadaver dog, leading law enforcement to the victims of crimes."

He stopped where a bookcase had been pushed against the wall, and pulled another sherd from the top of a row of books. "Here's the other sherd I hid from Archie. It's possible that if the items in those bins had a very similar scent to the sherds, the greater concentration there could have distracted him from these items."

He walked up to the edge of the dais and handed the second sherd to Ed. "Professor Suleiman? Would you like to talk about these artifacts?"

I stood at the edge of the stage, one eye on Rochester, but he had moved over to Justin and settled by the boy's side.

Ed jumped up on the dais and met Blake there, and they continued the rehearsed part of their presentation, about the difference between sherds and shards. Then they segued into what these pottery remnants could tell us about the culture, the food, and the commerce of the site where they were found.

"For example, we've learned that during a ceremony of betrothal, the girl's future husband would pour perfume on her head and bring her presents and provisions. This sherd comes from an ewer that might have been used for such a purpose."

He turned the projector on again and I flipped the lights off. "The incised decoration on the edge of this sherd shows two hands uniting. We can infer because one hand is slightly larger than the other that it represents a man and a woman making a connection."

He flipped to the next slide. "Now this piece has no decoration whatsoever, so we believe it was for ordinary household use. It probably came from a larger bowl, one used to feed a family."

He talked for a few more minutes, showing additional slides of what life was like in Mesopotamia. Then he motioned to me and I turned on the lights.

Ewan joined Ed and Blake on stage and thanked them, then thanked his students for coming. "We'll talk more about this presentation in class on Wednesday," he said, and everyone rose.

Ewan looked like he really wanted to hang out with Professor Suleiman, but he'd driven his students in his SUV so he had to get back.

Tamsen and Justin were among the last to leave. Justin didn't want to say goodbye to Rochester, but he grudgingly handed the leash to me and they walked off.

Joey came up to me then. "The stuff the dogs found. Did you put that there?"

I shook my head. "I have no idea how it got there. Have you ever looked under there?"

"Can't say I have. The dais was relatively intact—we only had to replace a few boards over to one side where there had been a leak. From where I was looking it seems like those bins were pretty far back."

"I agree."

"So even if we'd opened the doors I doubt we'd have seen anything unless we went crawling in there with flashlights."

"They're probably items that the monks left behind and forgot about," I said. "Remember, we found that whole stack of missals in a corner of the dormitory?"

He nodded. "And they left all those statues in the niches in the chapel, even though they could have taken them away."

We walked back inside, Rochester at my heels, and went up to where Ed and Blake stood on the dais. Archie lay on his side on the wooden dais, but he jumped up as Rochester approached. He stood on the edge and leaned down to sniff Rochester, as if they were meeting for the first time.

Then he jumped down and he and Rochester play-fought for a minute, then settled in a heap together. "Archie knows that he's off duty now," Blake said. "So he's free to play or relax."

Ed held up the beads from the first bin that Archie and Rochester had found and they glinted in the light from one of the stained-glass windows.

"There's a tag attached to these beads which indicates that they are from the collection at the Belden Museum of Mesopotamian Art in New York City," Ed said. "I can't confirm the provenance right now, but there was a significant theft from the Belden Museum four years ago."

I caught my breath and looked at Joey, who appeared as startled as I was. Stolen goods hidden away on the property we managed? How come we had no idea they were there?

Then I remembered what Joey had said. We'd never investigated the area under the dais. What if there was more stuff hidden there? Or at other places around the property?

Joey turned to me and spoke in a low voice. "You don't think they'll suspect us, do you?"

That caused my blood pressure to jump up even further. Who had access to every nook and cranny at Friar Lake? Joey and I did. And who had a criminal record?

I did.

Even though I hadn't gone to prison for theft, many of the

inmates I met had been arrested for a wide variety of offenses. A carjacker had also been a burglar. A recovering drug addict had committed a wide range of petty crimes to support his habit. There was no reason why a hacker couldn't be accused of theft.

How in the world was I going to deal with this?

Chapter 11

Who Had Access

"Can you help me and Blake carry these boxes back to your office?" Ed asked.

"Sure. Joey can get a hand truck."

Ed shook his head. "We need to be very careful with these. But before we go, I want to see if there's anything else under there."

Joey kept a small, high-intensity flashlight on his keychain, and he handed that to Ed, who stepped down from the dais. He pulled off his loden-cloth jacket and handed it to Blake, then got down on the floor and crawled under the dais with a flashlight.

I hunched down and tried to look over his back at where I could see the beam of the flashlight moving around. "You see anything else there?" I asked.

He backed out. "Not right now. But someone's going to have to do a much more thorough search of your property."

I didn't like the sound of that. He stood, and we picked up one plastic bin while Blake and Joey took the other. We walked carefully down the aisle to the front door. Rochester and Archie followed, the yellow lab more willing to play with Rochester, and the two of them ran around a few times.

My office was plenty big enough for me and Rochester, but it was going to be a tight squeeze for four men, two dogs and two boxes. "Why don't we head to the classroom over there," I said, nodding toward the one closest to the chapel. "There'll be plenty of room there to unpack."

We left one bin on the floor and put the other on the table at the front of the room. I moved the teaching podium away and Ed began carefully unpacking, laying each item out on the table. I caught my breath at one necklace which was made of six strings of tiny gold beads. It shimmered in the fluorescent light of the classroom.

It took nearly an hour to unpack everything, one treasure after another. It was like having our own private museum unfold before us, and several times I saw Ed's mouth drop open in surprise.

He was the real expert—Joey, Blake and I were merely onlookers. Occasionally Ed would stop and hold something up. He showed us one piece, a plaque featuring the head of a bearded man wearing a flat cap. "This is Sargon the Great, the first ruler of the Akkadian empire. This was probably mounted on the wall of a tomb, perhaps to invoke Sargon's blessing. See these marks at the back? That's where a grave robber pried it away."

The word "robber" took me away for a moment. I had to remember that these were stolen goods, and that they'd been found at the property that I managed. I knew that I had nothing to do with the theft—but would I ever have to prove that?

Ed shook his head and reverently placed the head to the side. A few minutes later he held up a short, squat jar with painted decoration on the shoulder. "This is characteristic of the period around 3000 B.C. in Mesopotamia," he said. "These nubs here along the top are called lugs, and a string would have been tied through them to secure a top over the vessel."

It was a shame we hadn't been able to carry this out in front of the students—imagine what they would have learned! I could tell from the look on Joey's face that he was as much in awe as I was.

Then Ed showed us a plaque with images of people. "The seated man and woman at the top are celebrating at a banquet, perhaps after a wedding," he said. "The other figures are servants bringing them food and drink."

I smiled at the thought of servants bringing Lili and me food and drink at our wedding. Oh, yeah. In our era they were called waiters, and if we had a sit-down meal we'd have to have them, too.

It was weird the way my head kept jumping around as Ed showed us treasures from the two plastic bins. I admired them, and then they made me think of my own upcoming nuptials, and then I was reminded again that the items were stolen.

Ed pointed to a man carrying a jar. "That's probably filled with beer. Some historians believe that the ability to create alcohol on a regular basis was what led ancient people to begin cultivating grain."

He laughed. "Others will say it was for bread, but no one really knows. See this hole in the center? The purpose of this plaque was to be part of a door-locking system for important buildings. You'd embed this in the door jamb, and then a peg on a cord was inserted there. Then the building would be sealed until it was ready to open again."

The piece that most interested Rochester was a plaque that was a mosaic of a lion in full stride. "This piece would have been placed somewhere to honor Ishtar, the goddess of war, whose symbol was the lion," Ed said.

I thought the lion looked a bit like Rochester, though of course the lion was much fiercer.

In every case, the items had a tag indicating that they came from the Belden Museum in New York. "What do you think we should do now?" Blake asked Ed. "Call the museum?"

Ed shook his head. "This is beyond the museum. We need to call the FBI."

From the side of the room, I felt my shoulders sink. I'd had a couple of run-ins with the FBI in the past and I hadn't enjoyed them. And of course, with the artifacts found on the property I supervised, I was sure I'd be subject to a lot of questions.

Rochester has a very good sense of my moods, and as he'd gone to comfort Justin, he came over to me. I sat on one of the wooden chairs and stroked his head.

It was already late in the day, so Joey left us to walk around the property and shut everything down. Ed called an agent in the Philadelphia office that he had worked with in the past, and explained the situation to him.

They talked for a couple of minutes, and then he said, "Will do, Hank. Do you need directions to get here?"

The man called Hank said something, and Ed laughed. "Well, I suppose if you're a government worker you have to trust GPS, because it was invented by the Department of Defense. We'll see you in an hour or two."

The name Hank rang a bell with me. "Was that Special Agent Hank Quillian on the phone?" I asked.

Ed looked surprised. "You know Hank?"

"Let's just say our paths have crossed," I said. I had met Hank when a body was discovered on the grounds of Friar Lake as we were about to begin our renovation. Then later when a college friend of mine was murdered and the investigation into his death led to dodgy dealings at the investment firm where he worked, I'd had to share what I knew with Hank and his fellow agents.

I sent Joey home. There was no reason he had to hang around waiting for Hank Quillian. That left me, Ed, and Blake, along with Rochester and Archie in the classroom, still marveling over the artifacts.

Very carefully, Ed began packing the artifacts again, nestling them in the plastic boxes. "See you later, Sargon. Though by the time I see you again you'll be behind glass and I won't be able to hold you."

"This must be like a regular day at the office for you," I said. "You get to examine this kind of material all the time, don't you?"

He shook his head. "I'm a historian, not an archaeologist. By the time an item shows up at the museum, we already know where it came from, how old it is and what it was used for."

"Is that where radiocarbon dating comes in?"

He shook his head. "We can only use that for materials that were once part of a living organism. We can't date things like stone, metal, or pottery unless there is some organic material embedded or left as a residue."

He put down the object he was holding. "For pottery or tile, technicians use a method called rehydroxylation dating. As soon as a piece of ceramics comes out of a kiln, it immediately begins to recombine chemically with moisture from the environment. We can reverse that procedure by drying out a tiny specimen completely then comparing it to the original."

He began packing up again. "Of course, all that is done by scientists. I look at the objects and speculate about how they were used and what they can tell us about the culture."

At five o'clock Agent Quillian called Ed and said that due to an accident on I-95 he wasn't going to be with us until at least 6:30. When Ed hung up, I turned to Blake. "Can Archie eat pizza crusts?"

He smiled. "His favorite food."

"Rochester's too. Why don't I order us some pizza while we hang out here?"

I called a place I knew in downtown Leighville and they agreed to bring a couple of pies out to Friar Lake. It was an easy order for them because they often supplied pies to the women's lacrosse team when their practice ran late. I also texted Lili to let her know Rochester and I wouldn't be home for dinner.

Since there were comfortable chairs and sofas in the narthex, the end of the chapel on the other end of the nave by the front door, I suggested we lock up the classroom and head over there. I even had a bottle of white wine in the refrigerator in my office, so once the pizzas arrived we had our own little party—which helped me forget for a while that Special Agent Quillian was on his way.

The motion sensor light at the entrance to the parking lot kicked on when Quillian pulled in. I sent Ed, Blake, and Archie to greet

Quillian and take him over to the classroom while I cleaned up. Rochester and I joined them a few minutes later.

Quillian turned to me as I walked in. He was in his early thirties, with the kind of weathered, wary look I'd come to associate with ex-military guys. Even after a long day, his shirt and slacks were crisply pressed. "Good evening, Steve. I knew that I recognized the college name and I used my time stuck on the highway to do some research." He turned to Ed and Blake. "Steve and I have spoken a few times in the past."

I noticed Blake and Ed share a glance.

"Good to see you," I said, and shook his hand. He reached down to pet Rochester, who was happy to accept his affection. I hoped that meant I wasn't going to get into any trouble with Quillian because the artifacts had been under my control—even if I hadn't known they were there.

He sat on one of the wooden chairs and motioned me to one across from him. "Let's start with the basics," he said. "This property is owned by Eastern College, right? For how long?"

"The college was in negotiation with the order of monks that owned it for about a year, and we took possession in 2011."

"And who has had access since then?"

I laughed. "I couldn't even begin to compile a list. We had subcontractors and tradesmen working on the renovation. Carpenters, plumbers, electricians, HVAC guys. The county had a contractor who brought up the water line, and PECO ran power lines. Then we had a couple of hundred guests for the grand opening."

Hank frowned.

"Since then, we've had dozens of local residents and groups here, from the Realtors to the La Leche League. Faculty members and guests put on presentations for students. A couple of the college athletic teams have used the premises for practices when their regular fields are unavailable. Literally thousands of people have had access to this property since the theft Ed mentioned in 2011."

"Does anyone on your faculty have a connection to the museum where these items were stolen from?"

"I can't say, because I don't know most of the faculty or what their research interests are. But you could try the department of history and sociology first. I think we offer a single course in archaeology and another one in anthropology." I thought for a minute. "Then you could also try the department of political science. Someone there might be studying the Middle East."

"What about security on the property and the buildings?" Hank asked.

"We have an alarm system but it wasn't installed until shortly before we opened to the public. The monks didn't have much in the way of security at all beyond antiquated door locks you could trigger with a credit card. And there was a period of about a year after the Benedictines left and before Eastern took possession. At that time anybody driving along could have come onto the premises."

I sat back and thought for a minute. "I never witnessed it, but I've been told that after the monks left, some kids from the local high school came skinny dipping at the lake. And while we were under construction, Joey and I often found empty liquor bottles, beer cans, and used condoms around the property."

Hank shook his head as he made notes.

"As part of our initial planning, we were worried that this property is isolated and might be a target for vandals. As you might have noticed when you came in, the monks built a low stone wall all around the property. We thought about putting in an electrified fence but the college's risk management department told us that would open us up to lawsuits if anyone was injured."

I could tell from the way that Hank gripped his pen he wasn't happy at how exposed the property was, but Friar Lake was out in the country, a few miles from the campus, and only a single road led up the hill to us. We took the chance that most would-be vandals couldn't find their way in.

"Before we opened to the public, we installed an annunciator at the front gate to notify us if anyone drives onto the property, and we turn it on when we're closed. It sends an alert to my cell phone and to Joey's, as well as to the local police. We've only had a couple of breaches since then, and the police attributed them all to animals."

"What about individual buildings?" Hank asked.

"We have security cameras pointed at buildings, also with an alert if there is movement around them. But honestly, we disabled those alerts because deer kept setting them off. And each building has an alarm connected to the main system. In four years, we haven't had any significant breach of any building."

Hank looked up. "Really?"

I shrugged. "We occasionally have sleep-over events here. A couple of times we've had guests who were staying in the dormitories try to get into the chapel or the cafeteria late at night, after we've set the alarm. But either Joey or I are here when people stay overnight, so we've been able to shut things off without major incident."

"You aren't going to make this easy for me, are you?" Hank asked.

All I could do was shrug.

Chapter 12

Visitors at Friar Lake

W e helped Hank carry the artifacts to his car, and then signed a set of papers transferring custody of the stolen goods to the FBI. Then he, Ed, Blake and Archie all left to return to Philadelphia. I made sure all the doors were locked and the alarm was set, and then drove home with Rochester, who was sated with pizza crusts.

Once there, I had to explain the whole situation to Lili. Then I sat at the dining room table with my regular laptop, logged into my Eastern email account, and started cancelling all the events I had scheduled for the rest of the week. Fortunately there was nothing beyond a lacrosse practice and a couple of meetings that could be rescheduled or moved to the main campus.

I also sent an email to President Babson about what had happened that day, and I copied the college's legal counsel, Benjamin Luna. I didn't think that the college could be liable for what Rochester and Archie had found, but if there was any fallout, I wanted to be upfront with the administration as soon as possible.

Like any college, Eastern had had our share of criminal incidents. Most of them involved students who were drunk or got into fights.

79

Items had been stolen from dorm rooms and offices. One year there had been a rash of break-ins where hard drives were removed from classroom computers. Another year a thief had walked off with unattended purses from campus offices.

We had drug-related problems, too. Students had always been able to get hold of drugs, usually from a local seller. But with the Internet, they were able to get hold of all kinds of bad stuff without any local intervention, and then either sell it on to others or use it themselves, often with deadly consequences. But I couldn't recall any incidents that required the FBI to show up.

Other than the two that involved me, of course.

Notifying everyone was a tedious process and I was exhausted by the time I crawled into bed. Rochester snoozed by my side, and woke me up at first light for his morning walk. I was glad to get out early to avoid meeting any neighbors. With the FBI's involvement at Friar Lake I couldn't focus on the tree problems.

Joey and I were both on site at nine o'clock as three FBI vehicles rolled in—Hank in his car, followed by two SUVs with two techs each. "This is our evidence response team," Hank said. "They'll make sure that everything we collect can be used in court cases."

Like I didn't already know that. But it was important to stay on Hank's good side, because I didn't want him to look too closely at me. I had managed to stay on the right side of the law for the last few years under Rick's supervision. I knew from experience how anything I had done could be twisted around.

While they were getting set up, Blake arrived with Archie and I went over to greet them. "I'm not sure how effective Archie will be today," Blake said. "He hasn't finished his full training yet, and there are a lot of scents we haven't exposed him to. But if we can do anything to help the Bureau, we're here."

Two of the techs began stringing yellow tape around the chapel, while Hank led the other two inside. I followed with Rochester.

"Is that the tracking dog?" one of the techs asked. He was a stocky guy with a pock-marked face. I'd been introduced to him as Luis, and the other was a woman named Cathy.

"No, the yellow lab is the tracker," I said. "Rochester works here with me."

"Does he need to be in here?"

I shrugged. "He has a good nose and he's been able to find things in the past."

"But he didn't sense any of these items?" Cathy asked. She was a slim young woman in cargo pants and a vest with multiple pockets.

I shook my head. "Hard to say exactly. He was in the area when Archie signaled, but that could have just been him being nosy. He has a good sense of smell, but only for things he's been exposed to in the past."

They accepted Rochester's presence. I pointed out the area under the dais where Blake had found the two bins, and Cathy squirmed under there with a flashlight on her head and a couple of evidence bags in her pockets.

Then I showed Luis the loose statues where Blake had hidden the sherds the day before. He rocked one of the statues gently, and it popped out. With a sinking heart, I realized he was going to take out every one of the statues around the perimeter of the apse.

About an hour later, two cars came up the driveway, and Rochester woofed to let me know. I often said that we didn't need to turn on the annunciator during the day because we had him on duty. The weather had warmed, but there was still a hint of winter in the chilly breeze that blew down from the mountains to our north.

I got another bad feeling when I realized that President Babson was in the first car. I recognized the Tesla SUV he had bought recently, part of his commitment to a carbon-free Eastern College.

The guy who got out of the second car, a sleek BMW, was in a dark business suit like Hank Quillian. Rochester and I walked over to the parking lot.

"Good morning, Steve," Babson said. "And Rochester." He leaned down to pet the dog. "Who's a good boy?"

Rochester looked up at him with adoration, his tongue hanging out of his mouth.

Babson straightened up and wiped a bit of drool from his pants. "Is Rochester the one who found the materials yesterday?"

I shrugged. "He was with Archie, the yellow lab over there by the classroom building with his handler."

The other guy joined us. "This is Ben Luna," Babson said to me. "Our in-house counsel. I noticed that you copied him on your message last night. Good thinking."

I stuck my hand out. "Steve Levitan."

Luna shook it and looked around. "Did the FBI provide you with a search warrant?"

"Nope. Agent Quillian was here last night, and when he told me he'd be back this morning with a team I didn't know if I could ask for a warrant."

"Why don't the three of us sit down and you can explain what's been happening," Babson said.

I led them to my office, and Rochester settled down behind my desk. I told them the story, going slowly and starting with Ewan Stone's request, and the short time to get Professor Suleiman scheduled.

"Is that how things usually work here?" Luna asked. "Faculty ask for use of the facility and you grant it?"

I nodded. "We also rent out space to outside groups, like the Realtors, who host a monthly lunch here. I handle all the approvals and paperwork. Though if I feel the subject or the visitors might have negative implications to the College, I pass the request up to the director of facilities for approval."

Technically, Friar Lake was under Bobby Flett, the Director of Facilities, but everyone at Eastern knew it was Babson's pet project and the most important things went through him.

"And you check the credentials of people coming here?" Luna asked.

"When a faculty member reserves the space, it's his or her

responsibility to communicate with the speaker. In this case, Ewan knew Professor Suleiman personally. If a random community member wants to rent from us, I do the checking. We did have an incident last year."

"The neo-Nazis," Babson said.

"Yes. A Leighville resident inquired about using Friar Lake for a group meeting, but when I discovered the purpose of the group I turned them down. The resident then approached President Babson's office."

"And I turned him down, too," Babson said.

"In this case, we had a recognized academic coming to Friar Lake from a prominent university to provide a demonstration that would be of interest to students, and support Ewan's teaching," I said. "That was all I needed to hear."

"We're not concerned with Professor Suleiman," Babson said. "I pulled up his CV after I got your email. He's an excellent choice for a speaker, and I know that as a dog lover you were probably eager to set up the demonstration with the handler from the Working Dog Center."

"I was."

"My concern is that we don't know where these objects came from or how they got here," Luna said.

"Professor Suleiman posited a theory last night," I said. "Each of the items we examined were tagged as belonging to the collection of the Belden Museum in New York. He told us about a robbery there in 2011."

"Which was about the time we bought the property," Babson said. "So those could have been here before we were the legal owners."

"That will be tough to prove," Luna said. "The Bureau will want to see footage from your security cameras, I'm sure. In ordinary circumstances, the FBI would provide a search warrant to us, as a matter of courtesy. But you were certainly within your job description to allow the agent to visit last night. I imagine they'll have the proper warrants soon. Law enforcement is allowed to search any premises with the authorization of the person in charge."

The three of us went back outside, Rochester by my side, and I waved down Hank Quillian and introduced him to Ben Luna. The two of them walked off.

"You've done a great job here, Steve," Babson said. "I love to come out here and see the place busy. We're serving the college and the community." Then he looked around at all the crime scene tape. "How long do you think they'll be?"

"Hank said two or three days," I said.

"And then you'll need to clean up afterward," Babson said. "I doubt the FBI is going to leave everything neat and tidy for you."

It was not a good day for my heart, which sunk farther and farther into my chest. "Joey and I will manage."

"I'm sure you will. But keep me and Ben in the loop with anything the Feds find."

"I will certainly do that."

He reached down and petted Rochester again. "You are doing good work here, too, Rochester. I only receive excellent reports on you."

This time my dog didn't drool on my boss. That was a positive.

Ben and Hank approached us, and this time Babson took Hank aside, leaving me with the attorney. "I doubt that it will be important in this case," Ben said. "But it is a matter of record on your employment application that you served some time in prison. Will that have any relevance here?"

My heart rate accelerated, and I took a moment to compose my thoughts. "In a moment of high personal drama, I made a bad decision," I said. "Mine was a victimless computer crime, and the judge recognized that in my sentencing. Since I returned to Pennsylvania I haven't done anything to bring me back into the view of law enforcement."

"But there have been incidents here," Ben said. "Didn't you discover a body on the premises?"

"Simply as part of an inspection before we took possession," I said. "And the victim had nothing do with the monastery or the college."

"You know, normally our hiring policy would prevent us from having a convicted felon in a position of fiduciary responsibility such as yours," he said. "President Babson must have a lot of faith in you."

It was time to play the alumni card. "He has always been good to me. But even more so, it's because I'm an Eastern alumnus myself and he believes in the education we provide and the kind of graduates we produce."

"Interesting. Well, keep my office informed of any developments out here."

He walked toward his car, and met Babson halfway there. They talked for a moment or two, then got into their respective cars and drove off.

I knew that Babson had made an exception to college hiring policy when he gave me my first full-time job at Eastern, in the alumni and development office. When I helped protect the college during a murder investigation, his faith in me had been solidified.

It didn't hurt that he liked Rochester, too.

But Ben's comments made me wonder if my time flying under the radar was coming to an end. As far as I knew, there was no law preventing me from holding my position at Eastern; it was only a matter of the college's hiring policy. But if it was discovered that the artifacts had been hidden at Eastern while I was in charge of Friar Lake, it might be my head on the chopping block.

And then I'd find it much harder to get another job, putting my future and my marriage to Lili in jeopardy.

Chapter 13

Personal Domain

Minutes after I settled down in my office to look through my emails, Joey came in. "There's a reporter outside from the *Courier-Times*," he said. "I tried to get rid of her with a no comment, but she said that she already knew about the theft, and that if she knows then at least one of the TV stations will be here soon."

"I'd better call Jodie Phillips," I said. Jodie was Eastern's Director of Media Outreach—what used to be called public relations. I had worked with her a few months before on the case of a student who had been caught plagiarizing.

"I've got a situation out here," I said. "With one reporter already on site and others supposedly on their way."

"Let me get my coat." I heard some rustling in the background. "I'm on my way to my car. Tell me what's up."

I explained what had happened. "Someone must have tipped the media off to the FBI presence here," I said. "I don't know what you want me to say to the press."

"Nothing until I get there," she said.

Rochester and I walked out to where the reporter, a young

woman in a Fair Isle sweater and a kilt skirt, was leaning against her car taking notes. I introduced myself. "I don't know what anyone here can tell you," I said. "This is an FBI case, as I'm sure you've already figured out from the presence of their vehicles."

"I'm Kelly Suarez. Tell me about this place, then," she said. "It's part of Eastern College?"

"It is. And Eastern's director of media outreach is on her way. She'll be the point person for you."

Rochester nosed against her, sniffing her legs, and she reached down to pet him. It was always a good sign when a visitor liked or tolerated, dogs. Lili's ex, freelance journalist Van Dryver, had never been a big fan of Rochester's, though they got along with each other. And Van had been instrumental in helping me uncover a dangerous dog-breeding operation in Pennsylvania Dutch Country some time before.

I didn't want to leave Kelly on her own while we waited for Jodie to arrive. In my experience, which I admit consisted mostly of knowing Van, reporters were sleazy, nosing in where they weren't wanted. They looked for any opportunity to trick you into saying something you shouldn't.

"Can I offer you a cup of coffee while you wait?" I asked. Better to have her in my office than roaming around Friar Lake unsupervised.

Kelly agreed, and Rochester and I led her back to my office, where I fixed her a cup of coffee and gave her the illustrated guide to Friar Lake that Lili and I had put together. While we waited for Jodie to arrive, I went through my emails and notified a few people and organizations that Friar Lake was going to be closed for a few days.

Jodie arrived about twenty minutes later. She wore a white polo shirt with the college's rising sun logo on the left breast, jeans and thigh-high leather boots, which Rochester wanted to lick. I had to grab him by the collar and move him back to my side of the desk, where I gave him a bone to chew.

I introduced Jodie to Kelly, and then shut the door to my office, leaving the reporter in the reception area. "What are we going to tell her?" I asked.

"We have to give her some information, or she'll suspect that something much bigger is going on. I'd say a statement like 'Some stolen goods were found at Friar Lake, which date back to the time before the College purchased the abbey. The FBI is investigating. That's all we know.'"

"Sounds good to me." I walked the two of them around the property as Jodie gave Kelly the formal statement. We stopped to speak with Hank Quillian, who had no comment, as expected. As we were finishing, a TV truck from one of the Philadelphia stations arrived.

"And the circus begins," Jodie said after Kelly walked away. "You'd better get accustomed to it. We're going to have a lot more visitors from the press here, or calls asking for information. But push everything off to me. If I want you to give a statement, we'll talk it over first."

"Got it."

We went through the same song-and-dance with the TV reporter, a young Black man named Trevor Reed. No, we had no idea where the stolen goods had come from. "Why is the FBI here, then?" Trevor asked. "They wouldn't be here unless there was an interstate connection."

"That's a great question," I said. "But I can't speak on behalf of the FBI. You'll have to get a statement from one of their representatives."

"Good answer," Jodie murmured to me, as Trevor went in search of Agent Quillian.

I barely made it back to my office after the TV truck had left before Joey came to find me. "Have you seen the chapel? They're tearing it apart."

I sat up in my chair. "What do you mean?"

"I can't be more literal if I try. Taking apart the whole dais. All the statues from the niches. It's a good thing the stone floor is original or they'd be prying that up, too."

"Are you going to be able to put everything back together?"

"I won't lie to you, Steve. It's going to be a big job. By the time they're finished we'll have a lot more to do than tidying up. Depending on how much damage they do, we might need a crew of carpenters for a couple of days to put the dais back together."

"Can you give me an estimate of how much it will cost? So I can scavenge through the budget and see if I can find some spare change?"

"Won't President Babson give you the money?"

"If I ask. But you know, we have to go through Facilities first, and they move like sloths in molasses."

He laughed, and mimed reaching a hand toward Rochester very, very slowly. The dog was totally confused, which made both of us laugh.

"What about anything else?" I asked. "We won't need roofers or electricians or plumbers, will we?"

"Depends on what they tear up."

"I suppose I should go out and take a look," I said. "I hope Rochester doesn't feel like they're destroying his property and start barking."

The three of us walked out. Two male agents I hadn't met, young guys in their late twenties, had set up a table in front of the chapel. Both of them wore the standard FBI uniform, dark suits and white shirts, though one had a blue tie and the other's was red and blue striped.

I noticed that Hank had brought back the bins he'd taken with him the evening before.

The guy with the blue tie was photographing the objects from the bins. The other adjusted the auxiliary equipment, including a big umbrella on one side and sophisticated lights on stands across from it.

A third agent, this one a woman in a similar suit, was adding detailed descriptions of each item to an iPad. "Her name is Joan, and she's the seizing agent," Joey said, pointing to her. "She keeps all the records of what they take away. I had to set her up with the site password so she can add information to her log."

We watched as she appeared to search her iPad for something, then do a complicated cut and paste.

I spotted Hank at the entry to the chapel, and as Joey went back to his office I walked over to Hank. "How's it going?" I asked. "How come you brought the bins back here this morning instead of leaving them at your office?"

"Whenever possible, we like to simplify the chain of custody. I locked them up at my house last night, and brought them back this morning so that if we find more items, they've all been photographed and notated at the same spot."

"Have you found more items?"

"So far we haven't found anything other than the items in the two bins," he said.

"Does that mean you can stop tearing apart the property?"

He shook his head. "Sorry, we have to do a thorough search. And I spoke to your attorney, by the way. I'll have a warrant to his office this afternoon."

A red-tailed hawk soared above us, hunting for rabbits or rodents or other prey. I felt like Hank was giving me the same scrutiny.

"I thought I was going to get in trouble for letting you in without one, but it seems I'm OK," I said.

"Well, if you're correct, the property we found has nothing to do with you personally or with the college."

I liked the way he hedged his sentence. If I was correct.

"Have you spoken to anyone at the museum in New York?" I asked.

"Yeah, they're sending someone down here this afternoon to ID their items."

"How about the media? Are you going to release the information that the items match what was taken from the museum?"

"Right now, we have no comment for the media. If the museum wants to make a statement, that's up to them. I spoke to your PR person and we're in agreement that neither of us will put out any information without showing it to the other first."

"One more thing. Will you be finished today?"

Hank shook his head. "We're not even done with the chapel. We have to go through the whole property."

My mouth opened involuntarily. "We just renovated this property four years ago. I don't have the budget to rebuild everything." I waved my hand toward the chapel. "I heard what you're doing in there."

"It's not so bad," he said. "Come on, I'll show you."

In the distance, I saw the hawk swoop down at the edge of the tree line and felt sorry for whatever the bird had gotten in his sights. But then, he or she wouldn't go hungry, and there might be chicks in a nest somewhere who needed to be fed. The circle of life.

I pulled open the heavy wooden door to the chapel. At first glance, the inside looked like a storm had blown through it. But then I realized that Hank's agents had been careful. Yes, they'd pulled all the statues out of their niches, but they'd only taken up half the floorboards of the dais. They had moved all the chairs around, but they hadn't ripped out the upholstery.

"The dog hasn't alerted us to anything in any of the other buildings so far. And we have no reason to believe that material from other crimes has been stored here. So we'll be gentle with your other buildings."

That was somewhat reassuring.

Rochester and I left Hank behind and walked out to the edge of the woods, where I let Rochester run free. He startled a squirrel, who scampered up a nearby tree. Rochester peed on the tree's trunk, a kind of 'so there' to the little furry-tailed rodent.

I felt a similar sense of ownership of Friar Lake, and I wasn't happy that I had to cede control of the property, even temporarily, to the FBI. I also felt violated—someone had brought stolen goods to Friar Lake and secreted them. Most likely, they'd been hoping that the market would cool off, and they'd be able to benefit from their crime without undue risk, perhaps never getting caught.

I had a strong sense of justice, even though I was a felon myself, and I didn't like to see anyone go unpunished. After all, I'd done my time. Why shouldn't every other Jack and Jill who fell down the hill unlawfully do the same?

Rochester and I continued to walk the perimeter of the property. The abbey had been built on top of a hill, and Eastern College owned all the land around it. The back end descended sharply to the street, though I rarely went back there because the descent was so sharp. A farmer's property picked up where ours let off.

On our circuit back to my office, I spotted Blake and Archie through the glass door of the farthest building, which was two stories. The main entrance led to a hallway with classrooms on either side. A central staircase rose to the second floor, where we had installed twelve single guest rooms, each with an en-suite bathroom.

We walked over there and stepped inside. Blake was waiting patiently outside the door to the first classroom on the left while Archie sniffed around. "How's he doing?" I asked.

"He's getting frustrated because he hasn't found anything. But I hid one of the sherds from yesterday in the room next door so he'll get a reward."

Rochester was straining at his leash, eager to get into the classroom and join Archie. "Can I let Rochester in with him?"

Blake shrugged. "Sure. I doubt he'll find anything."

I unhooked Rochester's leash and he rushed into the classroom. "What was this building originally?" Blake asked.

"As far as we can tell from the old drawings, this was the called the west range," I said. "This level was the domain of the cellarer, essentially the supply manager for the abbey. Those cabinets on the far wall, for example, are all original. They would have been used to store dry provisions. Guests were lodged on the second floor, and we kept the original staircase over there."

Then I pointed to the far end of the building. "There is an old well outside this room, which is where the monks got their water. It was still usable when we bought the property, but we capped the well because it was a safety hazard, and tied into the county water line that runs along the street at the foot of the hill."

I looked into the classroom, where Rochester was mimicking Archie, sniffing along the ground. Archie stopped by the original wall of cabinets and sat his butt on the ground. Before he could bark, though, Rochester was right beside him, and he went up on his hind legs and barked for me.

A moment later Archie barked.

"You think they found something?" I asked.

"Only one way to tell." Blake walked into the room, with me behind him. He got down on the floor beside Archie and opened the cabinet, while I moved Rochester away and opened the door where he had been pointing. I figured someone had left some food behind after a class, and that's what he had sniffed.

I opened the cabinet, and it appeared empty. That was strange. I really expected there to be some moldy food product. I reached over Blake's head and felt around inside.

Blake stood up. "I couldn't find anything on the ground level. Do you think that was what Archie was alerting for?"

"I don't know." I reached far back into the cabinet and my fingers touched something like crumpled paper. "You have any kind of a bag with you?" I asked Blake.

"Sure. I've been carrying evidence bags in case we find something." He handed one to me and I stuck my hand inside it. Carefully I reached back into the cabinet. This time I touched something hard, then the crumpled paper.

I used the evidence bag to grasp the paper and pulled it out. Then Blake and I both laughed. It was a McDonald's bag, and all that was inside were a couple of cheeseburger wrappers and a paper case for French fries.

"I doubt they have McDonald's in the Fertile Crescent," Blake said. But he took the evidence bag from me and put it up to Archie's nose. The dog looked supremely uninterested.

"There was something else back there," I said. "Another bag?"

He gave it to me, and I pulled out a water bottle. I held it up to Archie, who sat down on his haunches once again and barked.

"I'll be a son of a gun," Blake said. "I have no idea why he matched to that scent." He looked down at the dog. "But I can see Archie's discouraged. I'll give him a treat anyway."

He pulled a tiny bone-shaped treat from a zippered fanny pack at his waist, and handed one to Archie, and one to Rochester.

I looked at the bottle, careful not to get my fingerprints on it, in case it turned out to be important. There was a faded logo on the bottom, a circle with the letters BC around the top, and LES around the bottom.

"That logo looks familiar to me but I can't remember where I've seen it," I said.

"I don't recognize it. Probably a sports team. Though I don't know why Archie would have alerted to it."

"I'll leave you to keep looking," I said. "I'm going to do some research."

I walked back to my office with Rochester, where I took a photo of the logo on the water bottle. Then I uploaded the photo to Google's image search option.

Google scanned for comparable images, and at the bottom of the first page I saw something I recognized.

"Uh-oh," I said to Rochester. "We'd better get Hank in here."

Chapter 14

Water Bottle

I found Hank outside the chapel, talking on his cell phone, and waited patiently until he was finished. "I found something you need to look at," I said. "Back at my office."

As we walked, I said, "Let's step back a bit. I met you almost four years ago, when Rochester discovered DeAndre Dawson's body down by the lake. Do you remember that?"

He nodded.

"I want to go back to 2011 with you," I continued. "At that point, the monastery had been closed down for a couple of years, and DeAndre used it as a hidey-hole when he got in trouble in New York."

"That's the way I remember it, too," he said. "Now, yesterday Ed Suleiman said the museum was robbed in 2011."

"That's correct. March 25 of that year."

We reached my office and I led the way inside, Rochester threading between me and Hank. I pointed to the bottle inside the evidence bag, which sat on my desk. "Archie alerted to this water bottle in one of the classrooms at the rear of the property."

He looked at it, then back at me. "Why?"

I shifted the monitor of my computer to show him the match Google had made. "That's the logo for the Brotherhood Center on the Lower East Side in Manhattan. It serves a diverse population of homeless men and women, veterans, and recovering drug addicts. A soup kitchen offers a hot lunch seven days a week and a counselor is available to talk and help navigate bureaucracy."

I could see the wheels turning in Hank's brain so I spared him the trouble. "DeAndre Dawson used to hang out at that center. He was friendly with an elderly monk who had lived here for a while, Brother Anselm. He drove the brother out here a couple of times, so that's what made him think this was a safe place to hide. Unfortunately it didn't work out that way."

"Do you think he left the water bottle here?"

"Either he did, or someone else connected with the center."

I sat down at my desk, and he took the chair across from me.

"Here's a thought," I said. "If DeAndre knew this property was deserted, then other criminals might have known about it too."

I waited for him to nod slightly, then I said, "So if whoever robbed the museum needed a place to stash these artifacts for a while, they might have considered this deserted property."

"But that was four years ago," Hank said. "Why wait so long to come back? And why didn't you discover the plastic bins holding the museum artifacts when you were renovating?"

"As to the first question, I can't speculate." Well, I could have, but it wasn't my business to do so. "As to the second question, according to Blake, those bins were six feet back under the dais. He had to crawl to get them."

I stretched my shoulders. "We did a lot of renovation work on this property, but the chapel was in good condition because the monks used it for prayer every day until they moved out. We made some structural repairs and refinished the floor but I can't recall that we ever went deep under the dais."

"Well, we're taking care of that for you," Hank said. "My search team will make sure there's nothing else hidden there."

"Can't you compare what's in the bin to what was stolen from the museum?"

Hank's smile was almost predatory. "As you yourself suggested, this property may have been known to criminals as a good hiding place. Who knows what else we might find if we look hard enough?"

He took custody of the water bottle and the McDonald's bag and went back to the chapel.

I sat back in my chair and thought about what we'd discussed. I liked Brother Macarius, the monk who ran the Brotherhood Center, and I knew that he accepted anyone in need without prejudice. It was quite possible that some criminals had been hanging out at the center, playing video games and drinking soda, and that without his knowledge a plot or two had been hatched. One of those plots might have involved a theft from the museum, and a remote location to hide the goods until they could be sold or ransomed back to the museum.

To verify that theory, I'd have to go up to New York and talk to Brother Macarius. But I'd see what Hank was going to do first.

Later that afternoon, a tall, cadaverously thin man and a short plump woman arrived in an old Ford sedan. They were introduced as Phil and Jeannette, the curators at the Belden Museum, and they had brought with them an inventory of everything that had been stolen during the break-in four years before.

I stood with Hank as they began comparing their list to what Joan the seizing agent had recorded. It was a very dull process, so I took Rochester for a long walk around the property. The dogwoods and the crabapples were beginning to bloom, and the pink and white blossoms of the star magnolias made a lovely backdrop to the pine trees behind them.

I loved to see Friar Lake come back to life after the winter. Blake and Archie finished their search of the property later that afternoon, and Blake and I said goodbye.

"It's been an interesting couple of days," Blake said. "Far from what I usually do."

"What is that?" I asked.

"I'm primarily a trainer at the Working Dog Center at Penn. Mostly I work with faculty members who want to see if a dog can be trained for a particular purpose, like sniffing out cancer in patients. I also do a lot with the Citizen Science program, where we train dogs and their handlers so that they can participate in research studies."

"That's so cool. Do you think Rochester could learn something like that?"

"Does he have a high reward drive? Respond very well to commands?"

I looked at Rochester, who was sprawled on the floor by my feet. He had a lot of great qualities, and he was certainly smarter than the average dog. But I'd seen his sister Daisy in action as a search and rescue dog, and I knew he'd never have the patience to go through repetitive training.

I sighed. I really wanted to do some kind of training with him, but I realized that was more for my sake than for his. He was perfectly happy living his life, and I couldn't see putting him to work.

"He's not the best at responding to commands," I admitted. "Sometimes he can be headstrong. And I'm afraid I already spoil him too much to engage his reward drive."

Blake reached down to scratch behind Rochester's ears. "Every dog has a purpose in this world," he said. "Sometimes that purpose is simply to love a family."

I knew Rochester had a greater purpose than that, and even though I thought Blake might understand, I wasn't going to get into my dog's crime-sniffing abilities. And Blake had already seen Rochester go to the same place Archie had alerted—and even go up on his hind legs to indicate the water bottle was in the higher cabinet.

"Yeah, he's very loved, and loving," I said. "Aren't you, boy?"

He hopped up and nuzzled me. He was smart enough to know that he didn't need any additional training to keep doing what he was doing.

By the end of the day, all the items from the chapel had been photographed and catalogued, and Phil and Jeannette left. Hank said that he and two of the agents would be back the next day to finish up.

"Do you think I could get started on repairs?"

"We're done with the chapel and the kitchen," Hank said. "And we haven't really done any damage anywhere else. But we would rather that you wait to begin repairs for a few days, in case we need to come back."

"You're shutting down my whole operation," I said.

"Not really. The only place we've found anything is the class-room building at the far end, and the chapel. We'll string tape around those two buildings and you can use the rest."

Joey came up to my office a few minutes later and I let him know what was going to happen. It had been a long day, and I was glad to see Hank and his crew depart so Joey and I could lock everything up behind them.

The only questions they left behind were the ones we'd started with: who hid that stolen merchandise in the chapel, why, and when?

Chapter 15

Offensive

Unfortunately, there was more drama waiting for me when I got home. The folks on Hi Neighbor had been out in force, both online and at the clubhouse, demanding answers. What was going to happen to our tree replacement program? Would we be able to get any of the money back from Tree-B-Gone? Did we have insurance against that loss? I realized I hadn't heard anything back from Jennifer about the performance bond.

"People get very upset when you lose their money," Lili said.

"I didn't lose the money," I said. "And as long as we have a performance bond, the HOA won't lose the money, either."

"Maybe you should log into Hi Neighbor and explain that, since no one else on the committee is."

"I will never stop telling you that you were right, and I shouldn't have gotten involved in this business," I said. "But I will make the post you suggest."

Before I did, though, I went through the committee report where we had suggested hiring Tree-B-Gone. I didn't see any mention of a performance bond there.

103

So I called Jennifer Dodge. "Sorry to bother you, but I've been reading the posts on Hi Neighbor," I said.

"So have I. They're terrible."

"Did you find out anything about whether we have a performance bond or not?"

"I haven't had a chance to ask Henry."

"Do you have his phone number? I'll call and ask him."

She gave it to me and I dialed it. The call went direct to voice mail, but as I was leaving a message Henry picked up. "Sorry, I've been leaving the answering machine on because so many people are calling to complain about this tree business."

"I may have a solution for you. Did Tree-B-Gone provide a performance bond before you signed the contract?"

"What's that?"

Was I dealing with a complete pack of idiots? I explained the concept to him as I had to Jennifer.

"I never heard of such a thing," he said. "But this is my first time on the board, and the first contract I've signed on behalf of the HOA."

"Didn't the property manager give you any advice?"

"Catalina? She's useless. She sits in the office on her fat ass all day and talks on the phone in Spanish."

I sighed. "Hold on a minute, Henry. Let me check something."

I switched over to my laptop and navigated to the home page for the River Bend Homeowners Association. Catalina LaPointe was listed as our manager, but she didn't have any of the letters after her name that I expected—either a Certified Property Manager (CPM), a certified manager of community associations (CMCA), or residential management professional (RMP). I had a bad feeling about that.

"Who hired Catalina?" I asked Henry.

"She was in place when I started. I guess Keystone Properties hired her."

Keystone was the company that the association hired.

"This is a bigger problem than I thought," I said. "Can you and I sit down for coffee tomorrow morning and I'll give you some advice?"

"I could use all the advice you can provide," Henry said.

We agreed to meet at the Chocolate Ear the next morning at eight, on my way to Friar Lake. Henry ran a physical therapy operation a few blocks from there, so it was convenient for him, too.

"This is a mess," I said to Lili when I hung up. "And it's a level of aggravation I don't need with everything going on at Friar Lake."

"Play with the dog," Lili said. "That always calms you down."

Rochester knew we were talking about him, and he came over to drool on my knee. I spent some time playing tug-a-rope with him, and I did feel better. I did some research for Henry that evening before bed, printing up standards for an HOA to go over with him. I didn't understand why he hadn't done this research himself, before taking on the board presidency.

Lili worked in the kitchen while I played with Rochester, and I heard her pulling down pots and pans and opening and closing the refrigerator, but I sat back, confident in the knowledge that something delicious was underway.

As I heard the oven door open and close, I rose and went into the kitchen. "Can I help you clean up?"

"That would be lovely."

I began washing the mixing bowl in the sink. "What are we having?"

"You tell me. What's the holiday?"

I thought for a minute. "St. Patrick's Day was last week. Are you making Irish soda bread?"

She made a buzzer noise. "Try again."

I concentrated but couldn't think of anything. We'd passed spring break, and Easter was still a few weeks away.

"I'll give you a hint. Lunar calendar."

"Oh. Purim? You're making hamantashen?"

"You got it." Purim had been one of my favorite holidays as a kid, because we got to dress up for the Purim carnival at the synagogue and eat hamantashen, one of my favorite treats. The holiday celebrated yet another victory of the Jews over antisemitism, this time when a man named Haman tried to convince the Persian king that he should execute all the Jews. Haman planned to steal all the property of the wealthy Jews.

Our people were saved by a beautiful woman named Esther, who had won a beauty contest to be the king's wife. When she told him that she was Jewish and would have to be killed along with her co-religionists, the king changed his mind and had Haman killed instead.

The cookies that Lili was baking were shaped like triangles, after the hat that Haman had allegedly worn. There was nothing in the Book of Esther, as far as I knew, about the pastries, or about the poppy-seed filling I loved, called "mun" in Yiddish. But I was happy to eat them when they came out of the oven. I even burned my tongue because I couldn't wait long enough, which Lili told me served me right.

Before we went to bed Lili and I watched the late news on the Philadelphia station that had sent a TV truck out to Friar Lake that afternoon.

Though it wouldn't have been evident to a casual viewer, Lili pointed out that Trevor Reed's report was a clever mashup of what he'd been able to see on site, and what his team had learned after he left. He reported that representatives of the Belden Museum in New York had arrived at Friar Lake that afternoon, and then summarized the 2011 theft. He left viewers with a teaser that they'd have more news on this developing story on Wednesday.

"If he wants more news he'll have to get it from Hank Quillian," I said. "And good luck to him with that."

Wednesday morning, Rochester and I had another run-in with Pete Szabo on his three-wheeled bike. "I've been asking around," he said. "Seems like you're a pretty nosy guy."

"You mean about the tree business? I'm just trying to help out."

He shook his head. "You have a criminal record for computer hacking. Bet nobody around here knows that."

That took me by surprise. I had been living in River Bend for five years by then, and no one had ever brought the question of my record up before. Suddenly my heart was racing and my mouth was dry.

"I did the crime and I did the time. That doesn't have any bearing on my life today."

"I don't agree. I think it's high time the neighborhood knows what kind of man you are."

Rochester sat on his haunches and showed Pete his teeth. "We all have secrets, Pete," I said. "I'm sure you have a few you wouldn't like people to know about. If you're so sure I can find information about people, you ought to shut up before I dig into your background."

I don't know where that came from. I'm not normally the kind of guy to threaten someone. But between the tree problems and the stolen goods at Friar Lake I was on edge. I gave Rochester a tug on his leash and he stood up. "Let's get going, boy. There's a bad smell around here."

I was still shaken when I got to the Chocolate Ear to meet Henry. I didn't know if I wanted to drop off the tree commission or if I was going to stand up to Pete and let him say what he wanted. Or if I was going to do the digging into his life that I'd threatened.

But Henry didn't need to know any of that. I got my coffee and Rochester his biscuit, and sat in the dog-friendly part of the café. Henry got there a few minutes later, and once he had his coffee I handed him the paperwork I'd printed out.

"First of all, Keystone is responsible for providing us with a qualified property manager. I did some searching online last night, and I discovered that Catalina is Klaus Brito's sister-in-law. And that her last job was as a night auditor at the Holiday Inn in Levittown."

Henry looked like he didn't understand.

"Catalina isn't qualified for her job," I said slowly. "If she was, she would have advised you to get a performance bond from Tree-B-Gone before you signed the contract. And if you look at some of the other problems the board is facing, they're usually things Catalina should have handled before they became problems. Like the duck removal."

"So you think this whole business is Catalina's fault?"

"The board needs to make a complaint to Keystone about her. Ask the other members what they think, and if they have other evidence that she's not doing her job. And not just that she paints her nails and speaks in Spanish on the phone."

"I never should have agreed to be the president," Henry said. "I don't know anything about property management."

"Why'd you run, then?"

"It was my wife's idea. She loves the ducks, and she was angry with the last board about the way they tried to get rid of them. She's the one who coined that phrase 'duck-chau.'"

I liked Henry, but I wasn't going to back down on my opinion. "My great-grandparents and a lot of aunts, uncles and cousins were wiped out in the Holocaust. To use the name of a concentration camp in the context of relocating ducks is to trivialize their deaths, and I find that really offensive."

He looked at me in surprise. "She was referring to the way they were putting the ducks in cages."

"Which refers to the way my relatives were put in trains and gas chambers. Not nice, Henry."

"I'm sorry you were offended. I'll tell my wife what you said and I'm sure she'll agree with you. It was thoughtless of her."

"Thank you. So now, as part of your fiduciary duty as president of the HOA, you need to start collecting evidence against Catalina so she can be replaced with someone qualified."

"What about the tree contract?"

"If we don't have a bond, the only way we get our money back is to find Vic Davis. I'll talk to Jennifer Dodge and figure out what we can report to the police. That puts us on the offensive, and that will be the first step in a lawsuit against his company. But that's going to take time."

Chapter 16

Oh, Those Kids

B y the time I arrived at Friar Lake on Wednesday morning, Hank Quillian wasn't there, but I spoke to one of the two remaining agents who said Hank was at the office in Philadelphia if I needed him.

I needed to get the FBI off the property and get back to normal operations, but I didn't tell him that.

As soon as I opened my college email, I found a link Jodie had sent me to a very short article in the *New York Times* regarding the Belden Museum theft. The reporter had spoken to Phil, the tall skinny curator, and confirmed that items stolen from the museum had been discovered at Friar Lake. Phil was very careful not to say that all items had been recovered, and that their process of identifying and cataloging what had been found was ongoing.

There was a nice squib in the article, probably cribbed from Wikipedia, about Our Lady of the Waters and its transition to the Friar Lake Conference Center at Eastern College.

I called Jodie. "We got a nice mention," I said.

"Well, they're one of the last bastions of honest journalism in the country, if not the world. The *New York Post* has the story too, but they've framed it more salaciously, accusing one of the monks of being involved in the theft."

"I'll bet that doesn't make the Benedictines happy."

"That's the advantage of a community that believes in silence," Jodie said. "When it was operational, Our Lady of the Waters was under the auspices of Saint Vincent Archabbey in Latrobe, Pennsylvania, out by Pittsburgh. So far I haven't seen any official response from them."

"Do we do anything now?"

"I don't think so. The media will be after the FBI and the Belden Museum for further comment."

After I hung up, I checked the website for the Belden and saw that they were open on Saturday. I called Lili. "You interested in a trip to New York this weekend? I'd like to see this Belden Museum myself. I was thinking we could go there, then have dinner with Tor and Sherri. We could come back after that if you want, or stay overnight."

"I think it's a good idea to get out of River Bend for a couple of days," Lili said. "You make plans with Tor and I'll make sure Tamsen can take Rochester for Saturday night. Then I'll find us a hotel."

"Sounds like a plan."

I called Tor. Our lives had taken a very different turn after graduation, and he'd gone on to great success on Wall Street. He had been the only friend to stand by me when I was in prison.

"Lili and I are coming up to the city this weekend," I said. "Any chance you and Sherri are free for dinner Saturday night?"

"We have nothing on the calendar, though I add you now."

Tor had been born and raised in Sweden, and his English was almost perfect. Occasionally he missed a word or gave something a funny pronunciation, and he didn't use contractions. "What is the reason for the visit?"

I told him about the stuff we'd found at Friar Lake, and the museum I wanted to visit. "This month, Lucia wants to be an archaeologist," he said. "Maybe she will want to see this museum and we will all join you."

"Bjorn must be what, fifteen? And Lucia thirteen?"

"Yes, they are both terrible teenagers. It is a good thing I love them so much."

We talked for a couple of minutes and he said he'd get back to me about the museum.

I wanted to talk to Hank about the water bottle, but I didn't want to nose around in his investigation. So I decided that our first stop in the city would be the Drop-In Center on the Lower East Side. I had met Father Macarius, the brother who ran the place, a couple of times and we'd always gotten along. Maybe he'd have some insight into who might have left the stolen goods at Friar Lake.

That afternoon Henry Meskin called me. "I spoke to Klaus Brito, the president of Keystone," he said. "He had no idea there was a problem at River Bend."

"I'm not surprised."

"He promised to look into what's going on with the tree company, and whether Catalina should have made sure we had a performance bond from Tree-B-Gone."

"That's good, Henry. That's a first step to getting this mess fixed."

"Brito wants to meet with me tomorrow," Henry said. "After he has a handle on things. Do you think you could join us?"

"My schedule's flexible. Let me know."

"I appreciate your help. And I told my wife what you said about duck-chau. She was very upset that someone would make that connection."

I wanted to ask what she expected when she coined the term, but I was polite. I still had to live in the community, after all. "We just go on, one day at a time," I said instead, and we said goodbye.

The two remaining FBI agents left on Wednesday afternoon, without finding anything else. Joey got a carpenter scheduled to come up to Friar Lake on Monday to help him with the major work in the chapel. In the meantime he'd handle a few other things that needed work.

It was a relief to have the property so quiet, though of course I missed the groups passing through and particularly the students. I had a master's degree in English from Columbia, so I was qualified to teach, and occasionally I picked up adjunct assignments from Eastern. I really enjoyed the student contact, though I wasn't a big fan of grading papers. You can't have one without the other, though.

There were more complaints on Hi Neighbor that evening, and when I passed the River Bend clubhouse the next morning on my way to work, I saw a clot of angry neighbors waiting for the management office to open. I hoped Catalina messed up enough that her brother-in-law would let her go—or move her to another unsuspecting property.

I was busy most of the day Thursday confirming uses of Friar Lake for the following week, and we let the girls' lacrosse team come back that afternoon to use the playing field. Fortunately I didn't have anyone scheduled for the chapel or the outlying classroom.

Henry called and asked if I could meet him and Klaus Brito at the Keystone office Friday morning. "It's on Stony Hill Road, near the McCaffrey's market," he said. "I'm meeting him at nine-thirty."

"I'll have to bring my dog with me," I said. "He goes to work with me, and I won't have time to circle back and pick him up."

"I'll check with Brito's secretary and let you know if there's a problem."

"Thanks. By the way I saw a bunch of people outside the clubhouse this morning. You know what that was about?"

"That Pete Szabo is a real rabble-rouser. He rounded up a bunch of neighbors to complain about every issue under the sun. Catalina locked herself in her office and wouldn't talk to any of them. Then I spoke to Joyce this afternoon, and she said Catalina had packed her stuff and left."

Joyce was the long-suffering secretary, who had lasted through three property managers so far.

"That's good news, isn't it?"

"It turns the pressure up on me," Henry said. "Though if an angry mob comes to my house or my office I'm calling the police. I don't care if I put my neighbors in jail at this point."

I understood how he felt. Fortunately when I got home Thursday evening there were no protesters anywhere, and I was able to walk Rochester without running into anyone.

Lili was busy grading student portfolios that night, so I sat at the dining room table with both my laptops and thought about what I could learn that would help either of the theft investigations.

I couldn't find any new information on Tree-B-Gone or Vic Davis, though, and I couldn't do anything about the stolen goods at Friar Lake until after I spoke with Brother Macarius on Saturday.

I had given up on searching and was watching some videos of Final Jeopardy! when Lili came to sit across from me.

"I'm worried about how much time you're spending with that laptop," she said.

"I'm not doing anything illegal. I promised you that, and I've kept that promise."

"I know. But temptation is a bad thing, and the more time you spend with your hacker tools the more likely it is that you'll succumb. I've found real happiness with you, Steve, and I'm not going to let you steal that from me because you get caught up in your online world."

I sat back and tried to process what she was saying. Was I stealing anything from her by spending so much time searching for information online? Certainly, if I broke the law and got caught, it would have major ramifications not just for me, but for her.

Rochester rose from his place on the floor and rested his head on Lili's knee, as if he knew which side he was on.

"You're right, as always," I said. I turned the laptop off and closed it. "I'll put this back in the attic."

"I'm not trying to stop you from searching," she said. "I know that's an important part of the way that you deal with the world, with the way that you help people. I want you to recognize that laptop is like the snake in the garden of Eden. If you listen to it long enough it'll make you do things you shouldn't."

I reached over and took her hand and squeezed it. "You're more important to me than any online snooping."

She squeezed back. "I know that, but it's good to hear you say it. Now, can I help you with the ladder?"

I laughed. "Sure. You can open the garage door for me."

I retrieved the ladder and carried it up to the second floor, and stuck the laptop back in its space on the attic floor. It would be there if I needed it, but I was going to resist using it as much as I could.

I took Rochester out for a long starlit walk along the back streets of River Bend. Times like that I really felt the connection between us. He walked easily beside me, the leash loose. When he wanted to stop, I did too, looking up at the moon or the way the oak branches framed the sky.

Rochester had come into my life when I needed him most, after the deaths of my unborn children and my prison sentence. I'd come back to Stewart's Crossing because I didn't have anywhere else to go. Running into Rick again, and then taking in Rochester, had been my first steps on reclaiming my life.

I had learned how transitory happiness could be, especially if I wasn't paying attention. If I'd been able to communicate better with Mary, I might never have resorted to hacking, though I was pretty sure our marriage would have ended at some point anyway. Now that I loved both Lili and Rochester, I could see how differently I'd felt back in California.

I couldn't go back and make things right, but I could move forward with the love I had, and cherish it. The terrible thing about loving a dog is knowing that you will probably outlive him. That made me want to spend as much time with Rochester as I could, to make sure that he knew he was loved. While he stopped to sniff something, I bent over and scratched behind his ears. "I love you, puppy," I whispered.

Friday morning, Rochester and I ran right into Malgorzata Stopnicki and her angry Westie. "I've been trying to talk to you," she said. She turned to the dog. "Mishu! Hush."

The dog sat on its butt but kept a wary eye on Rochester, who stayed beside me.

"How can I help you?" I said politely.

"You people are blaming everything on my son," she said. "He's had some problems, but he's a good boy."

"Your son? Who's that?"

"My boy Victor. Victor Davis. His father was my second husband. A good enough man, but far too stoic. He never gave Victor the love he needed."

"So he made up for it by stealing a hundred grand from the homeowners association?"

She stomped her cane on the ground. "He didn't steal it! He signed a contract. You can't accuse him of anything."

"From what I know, he sold his house, gave away his dog, and took his boat out of Fort Lauderdale," I said. "And no one has heard from him since. He going to sail up the Delaware River and live on his boat while he removes our trees?"

"You people!" she said. She tugged on the dog's leash and turned around. "Come on, Mishu."

So Victor Davis was Malgorzata's son. Was that how he knew we were looking for a tree company? It was something I had to bring up with Henry Meskin and Klaus Brito when I met them that morning.

Chapter 17

Depression Lifting

T he office for Keystone Properties was on the second floor of a retail center in an area that had been farmland when I was growing up. Now it was peppered with gated communities, strip shopping centers, and a few remnants of the old times, like the Lower Bucks Masonic Hall, which had once been all alone, and now was surrounded by white fences and houses.

I let Rochester pee before we climbed the outside stair to the Keystone office, and met Henry in the waiting room. "I hope there's no problem bringing him in," I said to the receptionist. "I don't like to leave him in the car."

"No, we're very dog-friendly here," she said. She twisted a photo on her desk around to show me a photo of her with two labs. "They're my babies."

"Very handsome," I said.

Klaus Brito came out from the back then, and we all shook hands, though he paid no attention to Rochester at all. He was very suave, in a tight-fitting black suit with a blood-red tie and a matching handkerchief in his pocket.

"I was very sorry, and very surprised, to hear about all the problems at River Bend," he said, when we were all sitting in his office, with Rochester on the floor beside me. "I took a closer look yesterday and realized that Catalina had not been communicating effectively with the rest of the team."

He made a few apologies and let us know that she was being moved to another property.

"Our real concern is about fiduciary duty," I said. "Apparently the board of directors signed a contract with Tree-B-Gone without requiring a performance bond. Was it Catalina's duty to review that contract and suggest that we get a bond?"

He sat back and steepled his fingers—never a good sign. "Well, the Commonwealth law is opaque when it comes to things like that. A property manager who handles sales and leasing must have a valid real estate license. But there's no requirement for education or training for someone in a position like Catalina's."

"Surely there's a job description from Keystone," I said.

"Homeowner association management is a new area for Keystone," he said. "In the past, we've been focused on land acquisition and development. But as it gets harder to find buildable property in this area, we've expanded."

"So the bottom line is she didn't have a job description and she didn't have any training for her job," I said. "I'm no attorney, but I believe that means River Bend can sue Keystone for the hundred thousand dollars we're out."

"Wait, please. Let's not talk about lawsuits yet. Keystone may be able to help with the tree removal situation. I can't promise anything yet, but I'm looking into solutions. We may be able to send one of our yard crews out to remove some of the trees. And we will certainly support you if you take legal action against Tree-B-Gone to recover your money."

We talked for a while longer, and it was clear that Brito was a savvy negotiator. Henry, Rochester, and I walked out together.

"Not a very successful meeting," Henry said. "But we're talking. And we got rid of Catalina."

"I'm worried that whoever he puts in her place won't have any training or licensing either," I said. "Does the board get to approve the manager?"

"I'll have to check."

"That's a good idea," I said. "We want to avoid future problems if we can."

"That is, if we can get this one resolved."

"Oh, there's one more interesting thing," I said. "Do you know Malgorzata Stopnicki?"

"The lady with the nasty Westie?" he asked.

"That's her. I spoke to her this morning and learned something interesting." I waited a beat. "Vic Davis of Tree-B-Gone is her son."

Henry's mouth opened in surprise, then he shut it and sighed. "My mother always said, the acorn doesn't fall far from the tree." Then he walked off to his car.

Rochester followed me to my SUV and after anointing a shrub again he climbed into the passenger seat. "You didn't have anything to say in there," I said to him.

He curved his back legs and settled into the seat. "Fine. Be like that," I said. I reached over and ruffled his hair. "You found that water bottle. That was useful."

He put his head down over his paws.

The rest of Friday moved slowly, and I spent a lot of time wandering around Friar Lake with Rochester, or staring at the mess inside the chapel. All the unfinished business I had hanging over my head depressed me.

I did some searching for HOA lawsuits against management companies, and the results didn't cheer me up. It was hard to establish that the company or its rep did anything wrong when the legal requirements were so vague. Should Catalina have advised the board to get a completion bond from Tree-B-Gone? It was "good practice," but it wasn't required. Keystone Properties, because of their history as a developer, should have known about that kind of bond, and someone from Keystone should have advised us to get one.

But "should have" doesn't win a lawsuit.

Friday evening Lili and I talked over our plans for New York at dinner. "I want to stop by the Drop-in Center on the Lower East Side before we meet Tor and his family," I said.

"Why?"

"Because of that water bottle. I want to know if Brother Macarius has any idea how it got to Friar Lake."

She frowned. "Isn't that something the FBI should be taking care of?"

I laughed. "Macarius is a reformed ex-con, like me, so I don't think he'll be very comfortable talking to Hank Quillian. I'm hoping he'll be more willing to talk to me."

"You do have a way with people." She smiled. "I happened to see you talking to that white-haired lady the other day."

"Malgorzata Stopnicki? Did I tell you that she's Vic Davis's mother?"

"The tree man?"

"Exactly. She probably suggested him to Jennifer Dodge. Though she must have known what a loser he is. Why bring him into the place where she lives?"

"Some people don't think things through," Lili said pointedly, and we moved on to other subjects.

Saturday morning Lili and I dropped Rochester off at Rick's for an overnight play date. Justin answered the door wearing a sleep shirt covered with a photo of the galaxy and star-spangled pajama bottoms. Rascal was barking and weaving between the kid's legs, and as soon as Rochester got inside both dogs ran off.

"Hey, Justin," I said. "Did you like the archaeology presentation at Friar Lake?"

"It was awesome," he said. "Especially the parts where the dog found stuff the man wasn't expecting."

We followed him into the kitchen, drawn by the aroma of coffee and cinnamon buns. He turned to face us when we got there, with

Tamsen in the background at the kitchen sink. "Do you think we could train Rascal to find stuff like that?"

"Different dogs have different skills," I said. "I think if you want to train Rascal, you should find something that he's already good at, and make him better."

"Like behaving," Tamsen called from behind her son. "And less barking."

Justin grabbed a cinnamon bun and started toward the living room. "On a plate, mister!" Tamsen called. "And with a napkin."

He returned, obeyed her, and then left.

"Want a cinnamon bun?" Tamsen asked. "I made plenty."

"I thought you'd never ask," I said, and pulled up a stool at the counter. Lili laughed and sat beside me.

"I thank God every day for Rascal," Tamsen said, as she sat across from us. "He tires Justin out. If he didn't I don't think I could live through the boy's childhood."

I bit into the cinnamon bun, which was pillowy and gooey. Heaven. "Where's Rick?"

"Running. His doctor wants him to lose weight."

Lili elbowed me. "You should go to his doctor."

I gave her an affronted look. "Rochester keeps me on the go," I said. And then I deliberately ate a big hunk of cinnamon bun and smiled.

Lili shook her head and laughed. We left the house a few minutes later, and I felt my depression lifting as we headed north to the city. I had spent some great years there, exercising my brain in graduate school, having fun with Tor, and even in the early days of dating Mary.

The skyscrapers represented a kind of freedom I'd never have again. Not that I wanted it—I was very happy with Lili and Rochester and our lives in Stewart's Crossing. But you can't help feeling nostalgic for those times.

I was able to park near the Brotherhood Center, and it was weird not having Rochester with me to sniff all the new and interesting smells. Lili and I walked together down the sidewalk, skirting bags of trash and open metal doors that led to basements.

Despite the graffiti on the walls, there was a vibrancy to the neighborhood that I missed, living in a manicured place like River Bend. The buildings huddled together in the shadow of the Williamsburg Bridge. Some were freshly painted in orange and yellow, while others were white-washed brick or rough stone. Fire escapes zigzagged up the fronts of apartment buildings with multicolored laundry hung out the windows.

The signs mingled Spanish words, Chinese ideograms, and Cyrillic characters, and I heard a polyglot mix of languages spoken or yelled around us as trucks were unloaded, kids zoomed past on scooters and bikes, and elderly women pushed rickety grocery carts.

The Brotherhood Center was an unassuming storefront sandwiched between a launderette and a locksmith. The glass windows were protected by roll-up grills, and had been painted with Christian symbols and inspirational quotes. "If it's meant to be, it's up to me," read one that I particularly agreed with.

Lili and I walked in, and it looked much like it had when I first visited, four years before. On one side, a young Latina with inch-long nails painted bright red was behind a scarred desk working at a computer, carefully using the pads of her fingers to type. Across from her, three young black men clustered around a TV set and a game system. Gunshots and panicked screams peppered the soundtrack.

The walls were decorated with the same mix of Christian material and inspirational posters. A crucifix was centered on the back wall. I recognized images of Saint Sebastian, pierced with arrows; the Virgin Mary; and the Pieta.

Brother Macarius was at a desk at the back, and he stood up to greet us. He was a muscular Black man with a shaved head. He wore a plain brown robe with a cowl neck, full sleeves, and a hood on the back. He had a single white cord wrapped around his waist in lieu of a belt.

"Well, well, well," he said. "Nice to see you again, Steve. Where's your canine companion?"

"This is my fiancée, Lili," I said. "She's riding shotgun today in Rochester's place. Lili, this is Brother Macarius."

I realized it was the first time I'd introduced Lili to someone as my fiancée. It was an odd sensation that reminded me of the time before my marriage to Mary.

"My pleasure," he said, and shook her hand. "What brings you both here?"

I had printed out a picture of the water bottle, and I showed it to Macarius. "Do you recognize this?"

"We'd better go in the back," he said. "Can I offer you both some tea?"

"That would be nice," Lili said. We followed Macarius into a cozy room at the back, furnished with a couple of oversized sofas and a squat black machine that dispensed hot or cold water. She and I sat on a sofa while Macarius pulled out mugs.

"Oolong all right?"

"Fine with both of us," I said.

"Are you here on behalf of the FBI?" Macarius asked, as he poured the hot water over the tea bags.

"Nope. Just my own curiosity." He already knew about my affiliation with Eastern and Friar Lake, so I told him about finding the stolen artifacts in our chapel, and the water bottle and McDonald's bag in the cupboard.

"We ran out of those bottles about three years ago," Macarius said, as he brought us the mugs. "We had a grant for public outreach and that was one of the things we spent money on. As I told the gentleman from the FBI, we had about five thousand of those, and we gave them away at street fairs and to anyone who came in here."

I held the mug with both hands, waiting for it to cool. "So you can't make a connection between it and the stolen goods."

"I can't," he said. He turned to Lili. "We have a very diverse clientele here at the Brotherhood Center. Many of them, like Steve and I, have had run-ins with the law. We accept everyone as they present themselves to us. We help when we can. It would not surprise me to know that the thieves in your case came in here on occasion, four years ago. But I don't have any way of knowing who they were."

"Let me try another angle," I said. "The robbery took place at the Belden Museum on the Upper East Side. Does that ring any bells?"

He thought for a moment. Our tea had cooled, and Lili and I both took experimental sips. It had a slightly sweet, melon flavor and I inhaled deeply.

"I have a vague memory of that robbery," he said eventually. "As you can imagine, the clientele here often have an interest in criminal events. But no one ever took responsibility for it."

"Whoever stole the items from the museum left them at Friar Lake for four years," I said. "Can you think of any of your clients who disappeared soon after the robbery? I'm thinking maybe they were arrested for something else, which kept them from returning to pick up the goods."

Macarius stroked the cleft beneath his chin. "I can't think of anyone in particular," he said. "You know our clientele comes and goes, and unless we've placed them somewhere we don't know what's happened to them. It's possible too that the thieves never left."

"They planned to hide the items until it was easier to sell them," I said.

Macarius nodded. "People have short memories. You take an interior designer—four years ago he wouldn't touch one of those pieces because the theft would be in the news. But two or three or four years later? The market opens up."

We drank our tea and talked about the work of the Center. Macarius had taken an interest in an Eastern student whose family lived in the city, and I heard about him. I invited Macarius to come down to Leighville sometime for a visit, and he said he might take me up on that. Then Lili and I left.

"You have some very interesting acquaintances," she said as we walked back to the car.

"So do you."

"I was moved by how much Brother Macarius has accomplished on such a shoestring budget. I wonder if there's anything we can do to help," she said. "Maybe I can get Van to write a story about him and the work he's doing."

"Doesn't he write business stories?" I asked.

"I'll bet some fallen Wall Street types have passed through those doors," she said. "I'll drop him a line later."

The old Steve would have been jealous that Lili had thought of Van, but I reassured myself I was over that.

Chapter 18

Manhattan Interlude

My favorite street in Manhattan for driving was Park Avenue South, because it changed character so effortlessly from its origins in the still-Bohemian part of Greenwich Village, past Gramercy Park, where I had once lived with Tor, then onto the elegance of Park Avenue—and the tunnel beneath Grand Central and the viaduct around its side. That tunnel always made me feel like I was diving deep into the beating heart of the city.

Lili had found us a hotel on East 64th Street that had a parking garage attached, so we drove up there along streets thronged with weekend traffic. We left the car in the garage and walked a couple of blocks west to a café. There was something about the city that got into my blood and made me feel rejuvenated.

The Upper East Side was a very different place from Macarius's neighborhood. Here the buildings were beautifully maintained. Brownstones with flower boxes, doormen at the entrances to high-rises, elegant shops for the free-spending customer. Even the bike messengers seemed more polite.

We had lunch at a small café where every dish had an unfamiliar ingredient. Lacto-fermented koji syrup? Steak-and-egg tartare?

Streuseled bacon? *Quenelle de brochet* in lobster sauce? It made me want to order a simple hamburger, but instead I had a delicious cannellini bean stew with rosemary, which kept me warm for the rest of the afternoon.

Then we walked another few blocks north to the Belden Museum, an impressive pile on Fifth Avenue that had once been the mansion of the Belden family, who were early investors in Standard Oil.

We approached as Tor, Sherri and the kids came at it from the other side, and we all hugged and kissed. "You are going to be taller than your father, Bjorn," I said to Tor's son.

"Very soon," Tor said.

"And Lucia," Lili said. "You look like you're ready to start an archaeological expedition."

It was true; the girl wore the kind of khaki blouse and slacks I expected of an adventurer. She had round, red-framed glasses and perfect skin, and was going to be as beautiful as her mother—but I didn't say that. Girls and women get touchy when you talk about their looks.

The six of us trooped up to the museum, and as we walked in I spotted the plump woman who had come out to Friar Lake. "Jeannette?" I asked. "Steve Levitan. We met the other day at Friar Lake, the property I manage."

She came over and said hello, and I introduced my party. "Lucia has a particular interest in archaeology," I said, and the girl looked down shyly.

"Well, then, let me give you a tour," Jeanette said. We began at a map, where she pointed out the crescent shape of the region that curved around from the Persian Gulf to the Mediterranean. "This area was called Mesopotamia, and it's believed to be the very first region where people started clearing and modifying the land to grow newly domesticated plants as crops. That's why we call it the cradle of civilization."

I remembered what Ed Suleiman had said about growing grain to make beer, but I didn't repeat that.

She walked us through the main galleries, and I was pleased at the way Lucia, who'd always been shy, blossomed at her attention. Say what you will about gender roles, but it's always great to have an accomplished woman show a teen girl what she can do in the world.

Tor and I hung back at one point. "Why did you want to come here?" he asked.

I shrugged. "Curious to see where the stolen goods came from. It looks like they have pretty good security, though I'll bet a lot of it was installed after the theft."

Jeannette confirmed that when I asked her, as we were ending our tour. "Yes, the museum was not as careful as it could have been back before we were robbed. We had an alarm system, of course, but it was apparently easy to disable, and the thieves walked out with a lot of our most valuable small artifacts."

"Nothing came up for sale afterwards?" I asked.

"A few pieces here and there. But it's much harder to sell artifacts like these than your ordinary criminal might think. You can't walk into a pawn shop with a two-thousand-year-old gold coin and not get questioned about provenance. A few items did get pawned, but they popped up on the radar quickly."

"You weren't able to trace who pawned them?"

She shook her head. "All we ever got was that there were always two men, and they were African-American and very jittery, like they were on drugs. Nothing the police could follow up or narrow down." She smiled. "We're very grateful you were able to help us recover the items. We're going to create a gallery on the second floor to show them off."

We thanked Jeannette, and then went back to Tor and Sherri's for cocktails. They lived on the twelfth floor of a high rise, and the interior was very stark, with white walls and Scandinavian furniture. The art was what really made the place—big splashy abstract paintings in bright colors.

The kids went off to their rooms and Lili joined Sherri in the kitchen to "throw together" some appetizers. I followed Tor to his home office, where a nearly photorealistic painting of a Swedish landscape hung above his desk. To the right was a plaque from Columbia's Business School, thanking him for participating in a program. The school's logo was a stylized 4 with two horizontal lines beneath it.

"I never understood the meaning of that logo," I said, pointing to it. "Four?"

"It represents the staff carried by Hermes."

"Wasn't he the messenger of the gods? Seems like he'd be more appropriate as the mascot of the journalism school."

"But he is also the god of thieves," Tor said. "Hence the irony."

"Really? I didn't know that." I grabbed my phone and Googled Hermes. Sure enough, Hermes was the ancient Greek god of trade, wealth, luck, fertility, animal husbandry, sleep, language, thieves, and travel. "Certainly more than thieves," I said. "Trade, wealth and luck for starters."

"Ah, but you did not know the people I knew in B-school."

True. Though Tor and I were roommates, our friend groups did not cross over. Mine were literature and writing geeks, and we talked about the latest *New York Times* best-sellers, the proper use of the colon, and which of our professors were most likely to proposition students.

The only time I'd mingled with his friends was when Tor performed in the Follies, an amateur talent show put on by the MBA students. His specialty was parodying professors using the accent of the Swedish chef from the Muppets. Since he was Swedish himself, and could put on a heavy accent easily, it was a no-brainer for him. I didn't recognize most of the references in the show, but it was fun to see him sing and dance and generally make a fool of himself.

"How are things for you these days?" Tor asked, as he poured us both tiny glasses of aquavit.

"Good. I asked Lili to marry me, and she said yes."

He held up his glass in a toast, and we clinked them together. "Congratulations! She is an excellent person. And I like the relationship I see between you."

"What do you mean?"

"For a relationship to last, you need to be equals. You do not have to be the same person, but you have to have the same values and goals in life. Sherri is a type A personality, like me. When she decided she was done with modeling and wanted to move into real estate, I knew that she would become a top producer. And I was not jealous of her success—I applauded it."

"You've always been good that way. You're my second-best cheerleader. After Lili."

"Exactly. Mary had many wonderful qualities, and I understand why you married her, but she was not the right match for you. Lili is."

I thought so, too, but it was good to get the validation of my oldest friend as well. We went back to the living room, where Sherri and Lili offered us a platter of cheese, crackers, and tiny Swedish meatballs. As Tor headed to the bar to make drinks, Sherri said, "Do you have an announcement, Steve?"

I looked at Lili, who smiled. "I guess you both already know, then. Lili and I are getting married, most likely at Columbus Day weekend."

"That is so wonderful!" she said. Tor took our cocktail orders, and then we all sat together. Apparently Lili and Sherri had already begun discussing wedding details in the kitchen, and Tor and I listened and added our own ideas.

Eventually the kids called out for sushi and Tor, Sherri, Lili and I headed to a restaurant nearby. On the way, Sherri was talking animatedly, and not watching where she was going. She tripped over an uneven piece of sidewalk that had been pushed up by tree roots underneath.

Fortunately, Tor grabbed her arm, and she wasn't hurt. "That's exactly the kind of problem we're having at River Bend," I said. "But if Sherri had hurt herself, who could you go after? Not the city, for sure."

"But in your community, you are responsible for maintenance of the streets," Tor said. "So you may have a big lawsuit. I see why you are worried."

We had a great evening, and then Lili and I walked back to our boutique hotel. When I awoke the next morning I found a note from Lili that she'd gone out to take photographs, and I rolled over and went back to sleep.

She returned around ten with coffee, chocolate croissants, and a copy of the Sunday *Times*. We ate leisurely until Lili noticed an article entitled "Search Demonstration Uncovers Unexpected Results."

It was a follow-up to the short article about the return of the stolen items to the Belden Museum. "According to conversations with the FBI and city pawn shop employees, the thieves were thwarted in early attempts to sell some stolen items from the Belden," the article read. "Perhaps because of that, the thieves decided to hide them at an abandoned property in rural Pennsylvania. They didn't take into account that the Abbey of Our Lady of the Waters, which had been abandoned by the Benedictines, had been purchased by Eastern College for renovation into a conference center."

The article continued, "In a strange twist, Eastern Professor Ewan Stone learned that his graduate school mentor, Dr. Edwin Suleiman, had initiated a program at the University of Pennsylvania to train dogs to sniff out the scent of antiquities from the Fertile Crescent. He invited Suleiman to bring a handler and a dog to the college, outside Philadelphia, for a demonstration. According to Suleiman, he was surprised when the dog sniffed out the items stolen from the museum."

"I would have said 'astonished' rather than 'surprised.' Maybe even gobsmacked," I said.

"This is the *Times* from New York, not the one from London," Lili said.

I read more of the article out to her. "The FBI was contacted and the items returned to the Belden. According to a spokesman for the college, there is no apparent connection between Eastern and the theft from the museum. No students or faculty had any relationship with the museum, and it is believed that the items were hidden there before the college took possession of the property."

There was only one point in the article that I didn't already know. "According to Belden curators, the only item still missing is an 18th century diary by the German explorer Carsten Niebuhr, a member of the Royal Danish Arabia Expedition, which took place from 1761-1767."

"I didn't hear anyone, either from the museum or the FBI, mention a book," I said.

"Maybe they didn't think it was important," Lili said. "Or it was pawned after the theft."

"I suppose. And even if it's old, it wouldn't have had the same scent as the stuff that Archie found." I looked at Lili. "I wonder if it's still at Eastern somewhere."

"I thought the FBI searched the whole property."

"They did. But maybe they weren't looking for a book."

"I see that look in your eye, Mr. Levitan," Lili said. "The FBI tore apart Friar Lake. You've got to focus on putting it back together, not hunting for a phantom book."

"I know. But I might do some checking when we get home, in case it turns up in some collection with records online." I held up my hand. "Using my regular laptop, not the one from the attic."

We lingered at the hotel until checkout time, and then took one last walk, heading west toward Central Park. Lili wanted to check out a photography exhibit at the Arsenal, one of the two buildings that predated the construction of the park. She wasn't impressed, and we left soon after, meandering our way along city streets back to the parking garage.

It took a couple of turns to get us onto the FDR drive, which was surprisingly crowded and moving slowly. "It's Sunday afternoon," I said, as we inched down the FDR drive. "Why are all these people out in cars?"

"Maybe they're heading to Jersey City for the afternoon," Lili said.

I turned to look at her. "Why?"

She shrugged. "Just a guess. More likely there's an accident."

By the time we reached the Battery Park Underpass, the second of my favorite tunnels into the heart of the city, I was ready for the one-traffic-light world of Stewart's Crossing. "How did we live here for so long?" I asked in frustration. We still had to go up West Street to get to the Holland Tunnel.

"Because we lived in very constrained parts of the city," she said. "When you were at Columbia, did you stick around Morningside Heights, for the most part?"

"I did. And if we went to see a Broadway show, we took the subway. It was a big adventure to go to the Village."

"I was the same way when I studied at NYU, and then dropped out to live with Adriano. We never went anywhere we couldn't walk or take a cab. When I lived on the Upper East Side with Philip, we took car services everywhere. And even then, we probably never went north of 96th Street or south of Chinatown or Tribeca."

"So it's getting into and out of the city that's the problem," I said, as we moved somewhat more quickly up to the Holland Tunnel entrance.

"Hence the prejudice against the Bridge and Tunnel crowd," Lili said. "Keeping out the riffraff from Jersey and the outer boroughs."

"Not to mention Long Island," I said. "Or, as we used to say, Lawn Guyland."

It was funny that Lili and I shared the common history of life in the city, yet it rarely came up. She was three years older than I was, so when she was at NYU I was still in high school. But our time in the city had overlapped when she was working on her MFA in photography at NYU and I was at Columbia.

Then our lives had diverged—I married Mary and moved to California. Lili divorced Philip after a few years and took off on a round-the-world photojournalist career. But the world moved in mysterious ways, and it had brought us together in what the *Times* called "rural Pennsylvania."

We didn't talk much on the highway, and I was glad to exit I-295 and return to country roads. We got back to Stewart's Crossing around dusk, and heard Rochester bark as we walked up to Rick's door. He gave me a sheepish look that made he think he was embarrassed that he hadn't missed me at all, though he did jump up on my pants for a head-rub.

By the time we got home, it was clear he was tired after two days of activity with Rascal and Justin, and we took only a couple of very quick walks. The weather was warming, and it felt like spring would bring a new freshness. I was looking forward to cleaning up Friar Lake and moving forward with the academic year. I wasn't prepared for what I found on Monday morning, though.

Chapter 19

New Development

L ili and I had both ignored Hi Neighbor when we were in New York, and to further avoid trouble I roused Rochester early and we managed a pleasant if chilly walk. We got to Friar Lake at nine, and Joey came up to my car as I was parking.

"I've got a carpenter coming this afternoon to get started on repairs to the chapel," he said. "You want to go over there with me to make a list of what needs to be done?"

Rochester jumped out of the car behind me and stood there for a moment, his head erect and his nostrils quivering.

"Sure. Let me drop my messenger bag in the office."

Joey played with Rochester while I ran inside. "He's very antsy," Joey said. I noticed that he had one hand inside Rochester's harness. "He keeps sniffing and trying to run."

"You can let him go. He probably smells a squirrel or something."

As soon as Joey released his hold, Rochester rocketed away in the direction of the chapel. I marveled for a moment at how graceful he was in motion, the way his body moved with a singular purpose. This was the way his ancestors must have moved as they were trained to retrieve downed birds.

He reached the chapel door and turned back around to face us, barking.

"We're coming, puppy," I said. "Some of us only have two legs, you know."

When we reached the door, Joey pointed at the ornate metal lock, which had a big dent on one side. "Look at that," he said. "Why did the FBI bang on that lock? I opened the building for them every day."

"I don't think that was the FBI," I said. "It looks like someone who didn't know how simple the lock was took a hammer to it."

Because there wasn't much of value in the chapel, we'd never replaced the original lock the monks had used, a single bolt that could be turned from the inside, or locked from the outside with a large skeleton key that Joey and I both had copies of.

I pushed the door open gently, and Rochester rushed inside. "No!" I called. "Rochester! Come back here!"

Joey flicked on the light and I saw the big golden racing down the central aisle of the nave, toward the semi-circular apse at the end. But he skidded to a halt before the ruined dais, went down on all fours, and barked.

The stained-glass windows of the chapel let in a kaleidoscope of multi-colored light, but left the side walls in shadow. I wondered if an animal had gotten into the building while the lock was broken. It was possible that Rochester was confronted with a possum or a raccoon. I hoped it wasn't rabid.

It was ten degrees colder inside than it was outside in the sunshine. The chapel walls were carved stone, inside and out, and when we began renovations we decided not to cover them up with insulation and plaster. I pitied the Benedictines who had to flock there at two in the morning for matins and lauds. I hoped that their robes had been warm.

As I got closer to where Rochester waited, I saw a pair of feet, encased in running shoes, and legs leading to them. So a human rather than an animal. That was worse. I paused for a second, took a deep breath, then continued. I was in charge of the property, so it was my responsibility to know what was going on.

When I finally reached Rochester I saw a Black man in his thirties, wearing jeans and a gray hoodie. He was flat on the stone floor, his right arm stretched out away from his body. Blood had pooled around him with a long drip from what looked like a bullet wound in his neck. I knew that head wounds bled copiously, but that at the same time blood stopped flowing shortly after death.

I stopped short and Joey bumped into me. "Oh, no," I said. My mouth went dry and my heart rate began to accelerate.

Because the blood on the floor and on the man's neck was a dry maroon, I knew he had to be dead. I looked around the chapel quickly. Could the killer still be there? With a gun? Rochester remained on the floor, intent on the body, so I took that as a good sign. Surely if there was a live intruder, he'd be barking.

I felt Joey shivering next to me. "Do you recognize him?" he asked.

I forced myself to lean down and look at his face. Could he be an Eastern employee?

I stood back up. "I don't. Do you?"

Joey crossed himself and muttered something that was either Italian or Latin. "Not one of my landscape crew. And I'd remember that tattoo on the side of his neck."

We backed away a few feet, until all we could see was the dead man's feet. I called Rochester back to me, and he returned, sitting by my side. His warmth was comforting against my leg.

My hands were shaking as I pulled my phone from the side pocket of my khakis. It took me a couple of tries to find Tony Rinaldi's cell number in my contacts list. He was a police detective in Leighville who I'd worked with before when incidents had happened at the college.

"Hey, Steve, long time no see," he said. "What's up? You still have the FBI out there at Friar Lake?"

"No, they left on Wednesday." I could hear my voice shaking.

"We have a different visitor this morning." I took a deep breath. "A dead one."

"Did you call 9 1 1 ?"

"No, I started with you."

"Is there any indication that the killer is still around?"

I looked at Joey, who shook his head. "I don't think so. Rochester would be barking if there was a stranger on the property. The parking lot was empty when Joey and I got here, and Joey's already been around the property once this morning."

"All right. Don't touch anything. I'll be out there as soon as I can with backup."

I ended the call and then opened the camera app on my phone. Taking a deep breath, I leaned down and aimed the lens at the tattoo. I didn't know if it would be a clue or not, but I wanted to get a photo before the police came in and took over.

As I stood, I grabbed Rochester's collar and hoisted him onto all fours. "Back to the office, boy," I said.

He looked up at me.

I pointed toward the door. "You heard me."

He began trotting toward the front door, looking around behind him to make sure I followed. The inside of the chapel looked like a TV show crime scene. The planks that had made up the dais were laying haphazardly on the floor of the chancel, the space around the front of the altar. The carved heads that had been in niches in the wall of the nave now rested against the walls of the nave, in gruesome witness to the crime that had taken place.

The shadows along the walls of the chapel looked even more sinister against the bright sunlight that shone off the pews. The building had always been a warm, welcoming place, but now I couldn't wait to get out of it.

"I could use a good cup of tea to calm my nerves," I said to Joey as we walked out. "You?"

"Sure."

"Even though this is not the first dead body I've seen, it still really upsets me," I said. My hands were shaking. "I don't know who that guy is but what was he doing in the chapel?"

"Do you think he knew the first guy?" Joey asked. "The one who was buried down by the edge of the lake?"

As we headed to my office, I said, "I mentioned DeAndre Dawson to Agent Quillian because he was connected to the Brotherhood Center in New York."

"The logo on that old water bottle."

"Yup. The center is run by a couple of Benedictine monks, and DeAndre learned about Friar Lake from one of them who had been out here."

"Remind me about him, DeAndre," Joey said. "I hadn't started to work here then."

We were in my office by then, and Rochester settled on the floor beside me as I put two herbal tea bags in mugs, then filled them with hot water from the dispenser.

"DeAndre Dawson had a long criminal record, mostly for petty theft and drug sales," I said. "He spent two years in Sing Sing, and he'd only been on parole a couple of months before he died."

I added a packet of sugar to mine, but Joey declined and took the mug from me. Thinking of DeAndre reminded me that I'd been a parolee at the time of his death, and knowing what he'd been through had hit me hard back then.

"Because he thought I could relate to the ex-cons at the Brotherhood Center, Tony asked me to go up to New York and see what I could learn about DeAndre. He was a good kid until his mother, who was an addict, died of an overdose when he was in middle school. That's when his trouble started. He worked as a lookout for dealers, then started dealing himself."

"So he was out here to do a drug deal?" Joey asked.

I shook my head. "An elderly monk who lived here for a while told him about a relic that had been donated to the abbey. A gold chest that held the thumb of St. Roch, the patron saint of dogs. A rich patron had donated it to the abbey a hundred years ago, and this old

141

monk spun a tale for DeAndre about it. That the monks might have hidden it on the property and it was still here after they left."

Joey crossed himself once more, something I'd rarely seen him do. I remembered that he was Italian and had been raised a Catholic, though he only went to church at Easter and Christmas now.

"Do you remember Ka'Tar Winston, the boy with the two fingers on his right hand fused together?" I asked. "He was here for the summer program, and then came to Eastern as a student."

"Sure. I've met him a couple of times."

"He's DeAndre Dawson's half-brother. Same mother, different father. DeAndre convinced Ka'Tar to come out here that first summer. To get him out of the city."

"So he wasn't a completely bad guy."

"No, he wasn't. He had told one of the monks that if he found the reliquary with the thumb, he was going to sell it and donate the money to the Brotherhood Center."

"The guy who killed him was the same one who made trouble for Mark, wasn't he?"

I nodded. He'd had some minor acquaintance with the killer, through Mark, though of course Mark had nothing to do with any of the bad things that had happened. He'd been a victim as much as DeAndre had, though he'd gotten out alive.

Joey and I finished our tea as we heard the first police cars coming up the hill. I left Rochester in the office, to his dismay, and Joey and I walked back outside to wait for Tony to arrive with the cavalry.

"I have a carpenter coming to start the repairs this afternoon," Joey said. "I'd better cancel that." He walked back toward his office.

Two uniformed officers in a squad car arrived first. They must have been on patrol nearby. I explained the situation and the older officer asked, "Did you put the crime scene tape around the building?"

I shook my head. "That was the FBI. Long story."

The officer rested his hands on his hips. "This is the place where they found those stolen goods, right?"

"Yup."

His partner said, "We should go inside. To make sure the victim is dead."

I held out my hand. "Be my guest."

Tony arrived while they were inside. He was in his mid-forties, like Rick and I were, but he'd put on weight since the last time I'd seen him, and he was cultivating a mustache. "You have any idea who the victim is?" he asked, as he climbed out of his sedan.

"None whatsoever." As we walked toward the chapel, I gave him a quick rundown of what the FBI had been doing. "The *New York Times* ran an article about the theft and the recovery of the items yesterday," I said.

"Possible somebody read that and came to see if the Bureau had missed anything," Tony said. "Let's see what we've got."

The two officers came out as I walked over to the chapel with Tony. "He's dead all right," the older officer said.

"Thanks. You guys stay out here to make sure nobody who doesn't belong here gets in."

They walked back to the squad car and I led Tony up to the front door, where I pointed out the broken lock. "That's an oldie but goodie," he said.

"Yeah. Joey and I each have a key. We opened the door for the FBI each day, and I know that we locked up on Friday afternoon when we left."

The door was already open, so we walked inside and I led him down the aisle to where Rochester had found the body. With the door wide open, the room was brighter and it wasn't so creepy. It was still cold and I shivered. I stayed a few feet behind as Tony moved forward.

He knelt on the stone floor beside the man. "Looks like one bullet to the neck. Probably punctured his carotid artery. The carotids provide blood supply to the head and neck, and a wound like this usually results in massive hemorrhage leading to death within a matter of minutes."

"I still hate the thought of him dying here," I said. "Like there's something even worse about murdering someone on sacred ground."

"But this chapel was deconsecrated when the monks sold the property to Eastern, wasn't it?"

I shrugged. "I guess so. I was moved over here long after the deal was done. But don't you feel that there's still something holy here?"

The monks had dismantled the altar before selling the property, and removed all the obvious religious iconography. There was a broken piece of wood high on the back wall where I assumed a large crucifix had once been hung. The fourteen stained glass windows which I had learned depicted the stations of the cross were intact, and I assumed that the statues in the niches were replicas of saints.

"My father was a lapsed Catholic and my mother was brought up Baptist," Tony said. "So I don't get into religious stuff much."

We heard more vehicles pulling into the gravel parking lot and walked back outside. Another squad car had arrived along with an SUV for the crime scene team. While Stewart's Crossing had to rely on the county to provide investigators, Leighville was a larger town, with a much larger population, especially when the college was in session, so they had their own team.

"You can head back to your office," Tony said. "I'll come talk to you later."

I knew the first call I had to make, and I wasn't happy about it. I reached President Babson's secretary and asked if he was available.

"He's in a meeting with Mr. Luna," she said. "Is it urgent?"

"It is."

She put me on hold and a moment later I heard Babson's voice. "Steve? What's up?"

"Can you put me on speaker, please? Ben needs to hear this too."

A moment later I heard the ambient noise from his office. "This morning when I arrived at Friar Lake at nine o'clock, I discovered a dead body in the chapel." I was glad that my voice was no longer shaky. "I immediately called Detective Rinaldi from the Leighville Police, and he's here now with a crime scene team."

"Oh, my," Babson said. "My goodness. That's terrible news. Is there any indication if the body belongs to a student or an employee?"

"Joey's already indicated the man wasn't a member of his crew, and he's too old to be a student." I took a deep breath. "Black male, mid-thirties. Tattoo on the left side of his neck. It's a red heart wrapped in barbed wire, with flames rising from the top. Have either of you ever seen a faculty member or an employee with a tattoo like that? It's very visible."

"At last count we have over seven hundred people on staff, I make it a point to attend as many orientations as I can, and I can't recall any employee here at the college who has such a visible tattoo," Babson said. "Ben?"

"There are a couple of younger Black women who work in the dining hall who have visible tattoos," Ben said. "But I can't think of any men."

"Was there any indication of how this gentleman was killed?" Babson asked. "I'd hate to think we might have an active shooter on campus."

My nerves returned, and my voice was shaky again as I continued, "Bullet wound on the other side of the neck. I don't think there's any connection to the college, but I wouldn't blame you for being careful."

"We'll have to tread very delicately," Ben said. "A death like this is very grave. Even if it happened away from our campus, the poor man met his end on Eastern property."

"Why don't you contact the college chaplain and see what she suggests," Babson said. "If it's appropriate we can mark his passing in some way." I heard him take a deep breath. "Whoever he was, I'm sure there is someone out there who cares about him. The poor man."

"You have no idea what he was doing out at Friar Lake?" Ben asked. "You've had a lot of activity out there recently. Could his death be connected to the stolen artifacts?"

"There was an article in the *New York Times* yesterday about the recovery of the Belden Museum artifacts," I said. "That may have drawn someone out."

"I saw that article," Babson said. "At least they got our name right. The last time we were in the *Times* they called us Eastern State College." I heard him murmur something to Luna. Then he came back to me. "I'm sending Jodie Phillips out there. Keep me in the loop."

"I will, sir."

I hung up and called the college chaplain, as Babson had suggested. Deana Popescu had come to Eastern the year before. Though she was ordained as a minister in the United Church of Christ, her calling had led her to work with young people and she'd been an assistant director of religious and spiritual life at a larger university before coming to Eastern.

I wasn't sure how to address her – Deana? Reverend Popescu? Fortunately she answered her phone, "This is Deana. How can I help you?"

"Good morning," I said. "My name is Steve Levitan and I run the Friar Lake conference center. President Babson suggested I contact you."

I told her about the body, and she said, "I can understand that you and your staff must be very upset," she said. "You're sure this individual doesn't have a connection to the college?"

"Not yet," I said. "Right now no one recognizes him or his tattoo."

"It's hard to say what the appropriate response would be without knowing more," she said. "On the one hand, any death on Eastern property affects our whole community and should be marked. But there have been so many school shootings in the recent past, and I worry that announcing this man's death to the college immediately might cause unnecessary worry."

"What do you think we should do now?"

"Let me know as soon as you've identified the man, and if there's any connection to the college. If there is none, perhaps the best thing would be a brief memorial service at Friar Lake. That would be a way to honor his passing without making students worry that they are in danger. And if no one knew him, then there isn't a need to offer counseling. Unless of course you discover otherwise."

"Thank you," I said. "I'll let you know what we find out."

Jodie Philips called me from her car on her way to Friar Lake, and I filled her in on the discovery of the body that morning. Like everyone else I spoke with, she was upset to hear that someone had died, even if it was someone unknown to any of us. But quickly she shifted to the pragmatic.

"Do you think the murder and the theft are connected?"

"I can't say for certain. But the timing seems more than coincidental."

I hung up, and while I waited for her, I pulled up the picture I'd taken of the tattoo on the dead man's neck. I sent it to my computer, where I opened a photo manipulation program and enlarged it as much as I could.

I was hoping that there'd be a name on it, something that might help identify the victim, but there was none. I uploaded the picture to Google's image search function, and I got dozens of matches. Apparently such a heart wrapped in wire was a common tattoo.

I sat back and stared at it. "What do you think it means, boy?" I asked Rochester. "Barbed wire around a heart. The guy's heart was trapped by someone? And the flames shooting out the top? My love for you is fiery?"

He rose and rested his head on my leg. "Yes, I love you," I said, and I scratched behind his ears. "But I don't think I would get a tattoo for you. Or for Mama Lili, either."

Jodie Philips arrived about ten minutes later, and Rochester and I walked outside to meet her. He sniffed her running shoes, seeming disappointed that she'd swapped her leather boots for them. She petted his head and the three of us walked over together to where Tony stood outside the chapel.

She and Tony Rinaldi already knew each other from previous police investigations at the college. "Hey, Jodie," he said. "The techs took the victim's fingerprints, and we'll run them through the FBI's fingerprint database, but that can take a couple of hours."

"Any idea if he has a connection to the college?"

Tony shook his head. "You've got what, seven hundred employees?"

"Between faculty and staff, yeah," she said. "Any distinguishing features someone might recognize?"

I pulled out my phone. "He's got this tattoo on his neck," I said.

Jodie frowned. "Not very attractive, is it? Why don't you forward that photo to me and I'll send it to a couple of department heads in groundskeeping and maintenance, see if anyone recognizes it." She looked at Tony. "If I get any hits, I'll let you know immediately."

She held her phone in her hand until the email from me came through, then looked up at Tony. "Your people at the police will handle the press, right?"

"We will. Though they may come to you or Steve for background."

I looked down the hill, and saw a car approaching. "I wouldn't be surprised if that's Kelly Suarez from the *Courier-Times*. She was here when the FBI were searching the chapel last week."

"I'll take care of her," Jodie said, and she marched off toward the parking lot.

"Let's say there's a connection between the victim and the stolen goods," I said to Tony. "Maybe he was involved in the theft. Then why wait so long to come back here?"

"A couple of possibilities. First, he might have been in prison and had to wait for release. Second, he was waiting for people to forget about the theft so it would be easier to fence the stolen goods. Third, maybe it's that you're not the easiest place to reach and it took him a while to have access to a car."

"Then he saw the article in the *Times* about us finding the loot," I said.

"You think criminals read the *New York Times*?"

I shrugged. "I'm an ex-con and I do."

Chapter 20

The Uses of Pizza

J odie Phillips left, and Kelly Suarez came over to speak to Tony. "You know I can't tell you anything," he said. "You have to talk to our media liaison."

She shrugged. "Can't blame a girl for trying. Plus I like this place and it's nice to get out in the country."

"Do you ever speak to Eastern students about journalism?" I asked.

She turned to me. "No. Why do you ask?"

"We run a lot of programs out here, sometimes about careers. I can hook you up with the head of the career planning office. I'm sure students would love to hear about your job. I was an English major at Eastern myself, and I went to school with a bunch of people who went on to media jobs."

"Mine isn't particularly exciting, but yeah, I'd be happy to talk to students."

"Come to my office and I'll get you the information," I said. Behind her shoulder I saw Tony wink at me.

Back at my office I put Kelly in touch with my contact at the placement office, and we set up a program for a couple of weeks ahead. She promised to bring a photographer with her, and I said I would pass the information on to Lili in case she wanted to bring any of her students.

By the time Kelly and I walked back to the parking lot, the crime scene techs had finished and the medical examiner's people had taken the body away.

I found Tony by the side of the chapel, on his cell phone. When he finished, he said, "Thanks for getting Kelly off my back. She's very tenacious and she has a tendency to get in the way."

"No problem. Do you want me to go back to the Brotherhood Center?" I asked.

He turned to me. "Why there?"

I explained about the water bottle that Rochester had found while the FBI were on the property. "I'm sure this man's death has to be connected to the theft from the Belden Museum," I said. "Which is connected to the Brotherhood Center."

"That would mean we have to involve the FBI," he said.

I shrugged. "They're already involved. You want me to call Agent Quillian?"

"I'll do that. Hold off on doing anything until I speak with the FBI and we sort out who's responsible for what. The theft crossed state lines, so if the murder is connected to the theft it becomes a Federal case. But I'd rather investigate the murder myself."

"Whatever I can do to help," I said. "The way these guys used Friar Lake as their stash, that makes it personal for me. And I'd like to make sure that Eastern College doesn't get hurt."

"I understand. I'll get back to you."

I walked back to Joey's office. The old stone building smelled of motor oil and cut grass. He was sitting at his desk tinkering with the innards of a light fixture.

"I'm always impressed with the range of things you can fix," I said, as I sat across from him and Rochester settled on the floor. "You're a carpenter but you can handle anything electrical or mechanical. Did you learn this stuff hanging around your dad?"

Joe Capodilupo Senior had been the Director of Facilities for Eastern College until his retirement, and he'd mentored Joey.

"I guess," Joey said, sitting back. "He always said that the key to fixing anything was going slowly and paying attention. That once you mastered those skills you could apply them to whatever you were working on."

"My dad was like that. He had that engineering approach to everything." I shrugged. "Too bad I didn't inherit that from him. You would shudder to see the little cabinet I made in wood shop in junior high."

"I loved that class," Joey said. "And then electrical-mechanical shop the next year. I built my own basic computer in that class."

"The only thing I remember from that class was that you shouldn't unplug stuff by jerking on the cord. That you should grab the plug and pull it out of the socket that way."

"Well, at least you learned something."

"Tony's crew is finished with the chapel. What was the name of the carpentry company you used when you supervised the renovation? Maybe they're still in the system so we won't have to do new vendor paperwork."

"I did my apprenticeship as a carpenter for Bob Shakespeare, so he's an old pal."

"Why don't you give him a call, and then if he's got someone available to help you fix up the chapel, put together a purchase order."

"I'll do that. I'll walk back out to the chapel with you, so I can lay out the scope of work. I don't know if the FBI screwed with any of the electrical. And I want to see if I can fix the lock on the chapel door myself."

Rochester gamboled beside us as we walked. "You hear any other complaints about the tree work at River Bend?" I asked.

"Mark had a customer at the antique shop the other day who lives down the street from us. His maple tree is dropping pollen all over his car and he asked if I could come over and trim some branches, since the association isn't doing anything."

"Was he angry?"

"Not as far as Mark said. Just wanted to protect his car."

I left Joey in the chapel, and back at my office I hunted through the college's purchasing department files. Though Eastern had changed forms since Friar Lake was set up, another department had used Bob Shakespeare, so they had all the right approvals and insurance forms on file. I printed the information to use when filing the purchase order. Though Bob used Shakespeare and Company as a business name, the legal entity of the firm was Wooden Wonders.

Rochester and I walked back to Joey's office to let him know, and he said that he'd already spoken with Shakespeare and had a guy coming out that afternoon to look things over with him.

By the time I got back to my office, Tony Rinaldi was calling me. "We've been able to identify the deceased. Fingerprints showed up. His name is Rahim McCloud, and he has a rap sheet in New York for both robbery and burglary."

I didn't have to ask the difference—I'd spent enough time with Rick to know that when a victim was present for a theft it was a robbery; otherwise it was burglary.

"Can you tie him to the burglary at the Belden Museum?" I asked.

"Not yet. We have to get the FBI involved for that. But I was able to discover that the museum theft occurred during a period in 2011 when he was out on bail for another robbery in the same neighborhood in Manhattan. He was sent to Sing Sing in June 2011, and he was there until he was released three months ago."

"So that fits the timing," I said. "Let's say he robbed the Belden in March of 2011, then brought the stolen objects out to Friar Lake while it was still abandoned and unguarded. He must have thought this was a safe place to stow his loot while he was in prison."

"I spoke with Hank Quillian and he said that his office has

already spoken to someone at the Brotherhood Center and couldn't get anything useful. But you're free to go up there if you want."

"I've always found Brother Macarius very helpful, but I can imagine he and the rest of the staff are reluctant to reveal much information to the Bureau. I might be able to learn something more."

"Then go for it. You think you can go tomorrow?"

"Friar Lake is going to be shut down for the repairs to the chapel, so yeah, I can probably head up there."

When I hung up with him, I called the Brotherhood Center and asked to speak to Brother Macarius. I checked the clock, and it was almost twelve-thirty.

"Good afternoon, Brother. It's Steve Levitan."

I could hear the smile in his voice. "I had a feeling I'd be hearing from you again, once the FBI called me."

"I didn't get to bring Rochester with me when Lili and I came up, because she and I had other places to go. And I can tell he was disappointed."

This time the brother laughed. "You don't need an excuse to come by here, Steve. Our doors are always open."

"You think I could bring some pizza and soda with me?"

"That would make you even more welcome."

He gave me the name and number of a pizza place that delivered in the area, and I arranged to be at the Center around noon the next day, with food.

When I hung up I looked down at Rochester, who had recognized the word pizza. A bit of drool was already hanging from his mouth. "No pizza until tomorrow, boy. But we'll see if Brother Macarius and his crew are as responsive to a good pizza as you are, won't we?"

He woofed in agreement.

Chapter 21

A Mother's Love

I had brought a roast beef sandwich with me for lunch, and I poured Rochester some kibble from a package I kept at the office. While we ate, I caught up with the complaints on Hi Neighbor. Catalina, the HOA manager, had been reassigned to another community. "Good luck to whoever ends up with her," Pete Szabo had written.

One of the best (or worst, depending on your point of view) things about Hi Neighbor was that you had to be a resident of Stewart's Crossing in order to join. If your name was on the deed, the system could validate you easily. If you weren't you had to upload a document that showed a StewCross mailing address.

That's how Lili was able to join, because the house was still in my name only. That was something else we'd have to adjust once we were married.

We hadn't talked about any of those official items. I doubted she would change her name to mine. Mary had, because she hated her maiden name and was glad to get rid of it. But Lili was already established in her field. I already knew she didn't like the repeated L sounds in "Lili Levitan."

We'd have to change the title of the house, and we'd probably begin filing taxes jointly. Rick had told me that he got a better car insurance rate once he and Tamsen were covered under the same policy.

There was certainly a lot more to consider beyond when and where we would marry.

I went back to Hi Neighbor. You were free to choose your own avatar or screen name, though a simple click on the name you used revealed your real one. That was supposed to reduce spam messages and, according to the website, "lead to civil discourse."

The idea was that if your real name was attached to whatever you wrote, you'd think more carefully about it, and be wary of libeling someone by making unfounded threats or accusations. When it came to Tree-B-Gone, however, all pretense of civil discourse had been abandoned, and Jennifer Dodge had been accused of accepting a bribe from Vic Davis to hire Tree-B-Gone.

I was pleased to see that she had copied the definition of libel from Wikipedia, and posted it to the forum. "If you have direct evidence of this accusation, you need to present it," she wrote. "If not, I will be forwarding this post to my personal attorney... also known as my husband. And if you repeat these accusations orally, that qualifies as slander. So I hope you have been keeping your house in good order, because I'll be asking the court to award damages to me that will require you to hand that house over to me."

I was impressed. Especially because she ended her post with "Have a swell day," and two emojis. One was a house, and the other a smiley face.

I couldn't tell exactly how the neighbor had accused Jennifer, because I saw a message that read, "Original post removed by the poster."

Good for you, Jennifer, I thought. I copied her message into a file of my own so that in case anybody libeled me on the site I could use it, with minor modifications, of course.

After that, the language in posts was angry, if not specifically accusatory. Fortunately much of the anger was directed at Catalina and Keystone Properties. Henry Meskin had written a plea to give the HOA a chance to work out exactly what was going to happen, not only with Tree-B-Gone but with the tree removal work.

Rochester was bored, and he jumped up, putting his front paws on my desk. "What's with you?" I asked. "You've been outside almost all morning. You had lunch. What do you want?"

He pulled back, and a couple of the Shakespeare papers ended up on the floor. I leaned over and picked them up, and something clicked. Shakespeare had an official name, Wooden Wonders, and did business as Shakespeare Carpentry.

Was the same true of Tree-B-Gone?

Rochester slumped back to the floor as my fingers flew over the keyboard. It took some digging with the Commonwealth of Pennsylvania but the company behind Tree-B-Gone was called Davis Family, Inc., a Delaware corporation.

My mother had once worked for a business registered in the First State, and she'd explained to me that Delaware doesn't charge income tax on corporations registered in the state which didn't do business there. And shareholders who didn't live in Delaware didn't have to pay state taxes on share activity.

It wasn't much of a tax dodge, but some people used it. I continued to dig until I found the names of the corporate officers of Davis Family, Inc. The president was Victor Davis, and the vice president and treasurer were names I didn't recognize. But I did know the secretary. Malgorzata Nowak Davis Stopnicki.

Chapter 22

Involuntary Manslaughter

I called Rick and got his voice mail. "Can you meet me at the Chocolate Ear later? I have something I want to share with you."

A half-hour later I got a text back. "C U at 5."

I spent some time that afternoon researching Malgorzata. I found an interview with her on a website about the Solidarity movement that began at the Lenin Shipyard in Gdańsk, Poland, in 1980.

She had been born in Gdańsk in 1950, and graduated in 1972 from the university there with a degree in English. She went to work as an English teacher in Gdańsk, and in 1980 she began volunteering as a translator for news media. "I wanted to get out of Poland," she told the interviewer. "In my time, it was a very bad place. I had one skill, speaking English, and I was going to use it."

She worked for a number of American publications, and met a reporter from the Philadelphia *Inquirer* named Alan Davis. "I had to be very picky about who I worked with," she said in the profile. "Some writers, like the Jews, had their own agenda."

A Jewish agenda about Polish unions? What was that about? I looked at the photo Malgorzata had supplied, of her as a young woman, and I could see the same round facial structure she still had, though there was a craftiness in her smile.

When the government cracked down on Solidarity, she married Davis and moved to Philadelphia. "My husband went back to Poland for his job, and left me with a new baby and no one to help me," she said in the interview. "I cleaned toilets to feed my child. We divorced a year later."

That was all she revealed in the interview. I guessed that the baby was Vic Davis.

It took some more snooping in public records to find out that a year after her divorce from Alan Davis, she had married Wladyslaw Stopnicki, a fellow Pole, and moved to Port Richmond, a Polish enclave in the shadow of the Betsy Ross Bridge, northeast of Center City.

From a state teacher certification database, I discovered that she got a teaching certificate and became a high school English teacher at Our Lady of Port Richmond Regional Catholic School, where she taught until she retired until in 2010.

From another database I found that Wladyslaw died in 2009, though it was interesting that his obituary didn't mention a stepson. Real estate records showed that Malgorzata sold her Port Richmond rowhouse in 2010, and that she had moved into River Bend immediately afterward.

I sat back in my chair. What did that tell me? It was too far-fetched to think that she had moved to River Bend with the intent of aiding her son in deceiving the homeowners association. But it was possible that he'd visited her, heard about the tree problem from her and her neighbors, and seized the opportunity to cheat us.

By then it was time to leave for Stewart's Crossing. When I got to the Chocolate Ear, Rick was already seated in the dog-friendly part of the café with a cup of coffee in front of him that was almost empty. "Want another?" I asked as he and Rochester greeted each other.

"Decaf, please," he said. "This situation at River Bend is driving us crazy."

I hurried to place both our orders and return with Rochester's biscuit. "What's going on?"

"Your neighbors are going nuts," he said. "There are a couple of rabble-rousers on Hi Neighbor who have been rounding up people to protest at the management office. And this afternoon things got ugly."

I picked up my coffee. "Ugly how?"

"Name calling led to accusations. Which led to a man named Pete Szabo punching another man, Henry Meskin."

"Henry's the president of the HOA, and Pete Szabo is a pain in the ass."

"Then a woman got involved. I won't begin to guess at how to pronounce her first name, but her last name is Stopnicki. She whacked her cane at another neighbor, a man named Arnold Lafoon, and he fell and they had to call an ambulance. We had four uniformed officers out there to take names and issue citations, and the chief sent me out there to make sense of it all."

"The old woman you're talking about is Malgorzata Stopnicki," I said. "Also known as Malgorzata Davis Stopnicki."

"And that matters because..."

"Because she is the secretary of the corporation that owns Tree-B-Gone. Her son, Victor Davis, is the guy who ran out on the HOA with a hundred grand of our money."

Rick sipped his coffee. "Now it's starting to come together. Mrs. Stopnicki was defending the tree company, and Mr. Meskin was trying to shift the blame from the HOA to the management company. And apparently there's no on-site manager right now, only a secretary who locked herself in her office. She's the one who called 911."

"Joyce. Poor thing. Yeah, I met with the owner of the management company and he agreed that the manager had messed up because she didn't advise the board to get a bond that would protect the association if the contractor defaulted. I guess they haven't replaced her yet."

"I can't believe a bunch of grown men and women have gotten so upset over a bunch of trees," he said.

"It's more than a bunch of trees," I said. "It's a hundred grand of homeowner money that has gone missing."

His phone rang, and he answered it. "That's bad," he said, after listening for a moment. "I'll head over to River Bend in a few minutes and arrest her."

He ended the call and looked at me. "Mr. Lafoon hit his head on the pavement when he fell, after Mrs. Stopnicki hit him with her cane. They rushed him to the hospital but he didn't make it."

"Oh, no. That's terrible."

"So now I get to drive over to your neighborhood and arrest Mrs. Stopnicki on a charge of involuntary manslaughter. You can bet that this is going to make the news. Sweet-looking white-haired old lady kills an elderly neighbor. We have a dozen witnesses so there's no chance she can get out of it."

"But she didn't intend to kill him," I said.

"That's true. That's why it's involuntary manslaughter. Penalty can be a fine of up to ten grand, and up to five years in prison. Because of her age and the circumstances, I doubt she'll serve any time."

"As long as you're arresting her, can you charge her with anything related to her son's running off with our money? As a board member she has a fiduciary duty to the corporation."

"Unless you can prove that she knew what her son was up to, I doubt it. And once more, that kind of thing is investigated by the state, not the SCPD. You should let the president of the association know, and then he can pass that information to your attorney to use in pursuing restitution."

He finished the last of his coffee and stood. "Honestly, she'll have enough trouble with the manslaughter charge."

With one final pat to Rochester's head, Rick walked off toward the police station. I drove home and took Rochester for his walk.

As we passed Bob Freehl's house, he came out. "You hear what happened at the management office this afternoon?" he asked.

"Yeah. Malgorzata Stopnicki whacked Arnold Lafoon with her cane, and he fell and hit his head."

"I was there when the ambulance took him away. That made everyone stop arguing. But I think it's only going to get worse."

"It will," I said. "I heard that Arnold didn't survive the fall, and Malgorzata's going to be arrested for killing him."

"Whoa. And River Bend used to be such a nice place. I thought I left all this crime crap behind when I retired from the force."

"It's a sign of the times," I said. Rochester and I continued our walk, and when I got home I told Lili what had happened as we prepared dinner together.

"Were you ever in Poland?" I asked. Her work as a photojournalist had taken her around the world. "I did some research on Malgorzata and discovered that she was an interpreter for journalists during the Solidarity movement."

"I was fifteen in 1980," she said. "Living on Long Island."

"Oh, right."

"But I did encounter a lot of translators in various areas," she said. "They fell into two groups. The first were patriots who wanted to help us get their story out."

"And the second?"

"People who wanted to use their connections with us to further their own interests, whether it was for a political party or personal gain."

"Let me show you the article I found," I said. I got my iPad, and I took over stirring the pasta while she read.

"Interesting," she said, when she handed the iPad back to me.

"Which of your two groups do you think she fell into, based on what you read?" I asked.

"The second. The very fact that she married the journalist and left for the States. I wouldn't be surprised if she got pregnant while she was working with him, and then he had to marry her."

"That would make sense, considering they divorced almost as soon as she got here."

"Did you know the man who died?" she asked.

"Just to see him out when Rochester and I walk. And he was at the meeting where I spoke about the tree committee and he complained a lot. Apparently he tripped and fell over some tree roots and he wanted to sue the association."

"Do you think the woman who knocked him over can use that as her defense?" Lili asked. "That he was prone to falling, so it's not her fault that he fell?"

"Interesting. But I won't suggest it to her. She's been nasty to me and threatened me with the cane once."

"Good thing you didn't fall," she said. "I'd miss you, and so would Rochester."

He woofed in agreement.

Chapter 23

Nasty Words

L ater that evening, I was reading a mystery novel set in Venice when Rick called. "I arrested your neighbor this evening," he said. "It did not go well."

"Really? What happened?"

Rochester must have recognized Rick's voice on the phone, because he got up from the floor and jumped onto the sofa beside me. I stroked his fur as Rick spoke.

"I knocked very politely on her door, with two officers behind me. I asked her to confirm that she was Malgorzata Stopnicki, and she started cursing at me, and her little dog wouldn't stop barking. I finally had to talk over her to announce that she was under arrest for her part in the death of Arnold Lafoon. And do you know what she said?"

"Something very nasty, I'm sure."

"That he deserved to die because of the things he said about her son."

"Ouch."

"I asked her if she had someone to take care of the dog while I took her in for processing, and she said she wanted to take the dog with her. Of course that was a big no. She even insisted that he was her service dog, but she didn't have any paperwork to testify to that. When I told one of the officers to cuff her she started waving her cane around."

"Wow." I stopped petting Rochester and he looked up at me.

"I confiscated it because it's the murder weapon, and she kept yelling at me. I was glad when the officers led her off to the squad car. Before she left, she told me that her next-door neighbor has a key to her house, and he'd look after the dog."

"Just curious. Who's the neighbor?"

"A man named Pete Szabo. You know him?"

"I do. He rides a three-wheeled bicycle around River Bend." I took a breath. "He threatened me." Rochester sat up on his haunches beside me, and I scratched him behind his ears.

"Threatened you with what?"

"He nosed around and found out about my conviction in California, and my time in prison. He threatened to tell everyone in the neighborhood about me."

"Why would he do that?"

"Because he's a jerk? I don't know. I never had a problem with him before this whole tree situation."

"Well, he was very angry that we took his neighbor into custody. Started cursing me out, telling me that I had no right to arrest a disabled old woman."

Rochester settled down beside me again, on his back, with his head up against me. I scratched his belly.

"What did you do?" I asked.

"I told him that his neighbor's house was unlocked, and her dog was inside, and I walked away. To the accompaniment of many more choice words about my parentage and sexual behaviors. If the guy wasn't a sailor, he certainly hung around with a few to pick up all those curses."

I couldn't help laughing. "He really is a jerk," I said.

"Are you worried that he'll make trouble for you?" Rick asked.

I kept scratching Rochester's belly. "Everybody has something in their background they're not proud of," I said. "I've come to terms with what I did. I made a mistake and I took my punishment. If anybody wants to think less of me because of that it's on them, not on me."

"Good attitude."

"What's going to happen to Malgorzata?" I asked.

"I passed her over to the district attorney's office for charging. I'm sure I'll hear more tomorrow."

"You know, the only one I feel bad for is the dog," I said. "His name is Mishu. I'm sure that he's bad-tempered because he lives with her. I hope that Pete Szabo takes care of him."

"Figures you'd care more about the dog," Rick said. "Have a good night."

After he hung up I looked at Rochester. "Is that true, boy? That I care more about dogs than people?"

He rolled onto his back and waved his legs in the air. I certainly cared more about him than I did about most people.

Tuesday morning I drove to Friar Lake with Rochester, where Joey had managed to repair the lock on the chapel door. The guy from Shakespeare was already there, and the two of them were discussing how to approach fixing the dais.

Around ten, I called the pizza place Father Macarius had suggested and ordered a couple of pies and bottles of soda to be delivered to the Brotherhood Center at noon, and then I texted Hank Quillian to say I was on my way to the city. "Any questions you want me to ask?"

The message was delivered, but Hank didn't respond. Rochester and I got into the SUV. He was always eager to go anywhere, and despite the chill in the March air, I opened the window on his side so he could stick his head out.

I didn't mind paying for the pizza and soda. I appreciated the work the Center did, and because this was my second visit within a week, I wanted to stay on Brother Macarius's good side.

Rochester stuck his head out the window until we got onto the highway, when he curled up on the seat beside me and rested his head on his paws. When I traded in my ancient BMW for this SUV, I'd made sure the passenger seat was big enough to accommodate him. As they say on bumper stickers, dog was my co-pilot.

I rolled the windows up and we listened to a playlist of songs I had curated for the drive, starting with Elvis Presley and "Hound Dog." Rochester didn't seem to like it when I sang along to him. He sat up and stared at me, as if to tell me he was a golden retriever, not a hound dog.

He was happier with Cat Stevens and "I Love My Dog." Maybe because I didn't sing along. After that we had Toby Keith's "Every Dog Has Its Day" and John Hiatt's "My Dog and Me." New Jersey slid along past us as I tapped my steering wheel in time to the music. By the time we got Carrie Underwood's "The More Boys I Meet," we were cutting across the pendulous tip of Jersey that hung off above Staten Island.

I began to wonder why I had been so eager to return to the Brotherhood Center. I'd already been there a few days before and learned nothing useful. The FBI had spoken to Macarius and gotten nothing either.

Did I really feel that I was a better detective than the Special Agents who had been trained to interrogate and investigate? I was just a guy with a dog.

But I had learned to trust my instincts. I knew there was a connection between the center, the theft, and the death of Rahim McCloud. I was determined to find it. I also had a personal relationship with Macarius, based on our personal histories and our past encounters, and Rochester and I might be able to nose out something that the FBI had overlooked, or hadn't been privy to.

We emerged out of the Holland Tunnel to the Osborne Brothers singing about a Tennessee hound dog, and I turned the music off to concentrate on finding a parking space. Rochester was up on his hind legs and I lowered the window on his side. "Bark if you spot a place to park," I said.

Of course he was no help, focused on all the marvelous smells of the city. I found a barely legal spot a few blocks from the Brotherhood Center. Once I got out of the SUV I checked to make sure my back wheels weren't within the yellow marker on the pavement, and reassured, led Rochester onward.

We stopped many times on the way. "Two visits in one week," Brother Macarius said, when we finally arrived at the storefront. Rochester immediately moved up to sniff him and be petted. "And you brought this fine fellow this time."

"He missed out on our last trip," I said.

Macarius held his hand out flat in front of Rochester and said, "Sit," and my good boy immediately plopped his butt on the floor. Macarius pulled a biscuit out of his pocket and rewarded Rochester, who settled beside us.

There were a half-dozen guys in the room, as usual, watching TV and playing video games, as well as the staff and a couple of clients. The room had the same warm, welcoming tone I had seen before.

One of the desks along the wall was piled with random pieces of computer equipment. "Gifts?" I asked. "Or parts from defunct computers?"

"Both," Macarius said. "One of my success stories works for an Internet company a few blocks away, and he brings us pieces he thinks we can use. Someday maybe we'll be able to build a whole computer from them."

The pizzas arrived and Macarius laid them out on a table in front of the TV so everyone could dig in. "There should be one veggie, one pepperoni, one mushroom and sausage, and one extra cheese," I said.

The group expressed their thanks through full mouths. "Why don't we eat in my office," Macarius suggested, and I took a couple of slices and a bottle of water with me. Rochester followed eagerly.

I hoped that I'd learn something that would help Tony Rinaldi establish who killed Rahim McCloud. Despite the bad things I'd heard about him he was a human being whose life was snuffed out, an ex-con like me but who hadn't had the advantages I had. He deserved to have someone who cared about him.

In the end, though, this trip was all about me. As Lili had pointed out on several occasions, when I was investigating something I was like Rochester with a good scent trail to follow. I was relentless. That had gotten me into trouble in the past, but I kept pulling forward.

Chapter 24

Justice

"I appreciate the pizza, and the visit," Macarius said as we settled in the back room that served as his office. "But I'm sure there's another reason why you're here. Have something to do with Rahim McCloud?"

"It does. This is the second person with a connection to the Center who has shown up dead on the property I manage, and so his death resonates with me personally."

I handed a piece of crust to Rochester, who wolfed it down. "And as an ex-con myself I hate it when somebody isn't able to turn his life around after time inside."

"It took me a long time to realize that I can't save everyone," Macarius said between bites. "How did you know mushroom and sausage is my favorite topping?"

I shrugged. "It's mine, too. We get these pies in Stewart's Crossing, my hometown, with artisanal cheese and homemade sausage. You'll have to come out sometime so I can show it to you."

"I would like to see this Friar Lake," he said. "Since it keeps popping up."

He fed Rochester a piece of crust and took a drink. "So. Rahim

McCloud. I didn't know him well. He only came in here because it was a condition of his parole for a theft five or six years ago. We tried to get him into a trade program but he wasn't interested. He hung out for a while, like the guys out front, and then he disappeared. Took a few weeks before I heard he was back behind bars."

"That would have been in 2011, right?" I asked. "That's when he went to Sing Sing."

"If you say so. The years tend to blur together."

"Did he associate with anyone in particular?" I asked.

"Not that I can recall. But let me look up his record on my computer and see if there's anything interesting there."

He turned to his ancient computer and began typing, and I wondered if there was any way I could get him some new equipment. Eastern periodically sweeps through and replaces our computers with newer models. Older machines tended to break down more frequently, especially if the user didn't clear out unused software. Older models also might not be able to take advantage of new security measures, and those with limited hard drive space couldn't get the latest versions of software.

While I was thinking of that, my phone rang and I saw that it was Hank Quillian. "Hey, Hank," I said when I answered. "I'm here at the Brotherhood Center in Manhattan with my friend Brother Macarius."

"Good. Can you ask him if a guy named Lafontaine Delius ever came through there?"

Macarius had stopped searching to look at me. I repeated the name to him, and he asked me to spell it. "Let me put you on speaker, Hank," I said.

Hank spelled the name, and Macarius searched. "Yes, he was here in 2011," he said, after a moment. "Around the same time as Rahim McCloud."

"Who is Delius?" I asked Hank.

"He and McCloud robbed a liquor store on the Upper East Side,"

Hank said. "That's the crime that sent them both to Sing Sing." He thanked us both and ended the call.

Rochester was on his haunches, staring eagerly at me, so I picked up my second piece of pizza, took a bite, then broke off a piece of crust for him.

"We don't operate as a place for criminals to meet each other and plan their next crime," Macarius said.

"I don't think you do. But you can't control who talks to who, or what they come up with together."

He picked up his second piece of pizza and started to eat. "I hate it when we can't help someone," he said. He looked back at his screen. "Oh. I remember this guy now. He never used the name Lafontaine. His nickname was Grantay—which means tall in Creole. He was a big guy, six-four, very muscular. The kind of guy who wears muscle Ts even in the winter so you can see his guns."

I pulled out my phone and started to take notes. "Anything else you can tell me?"

"Very big personality, as you can imagine. Got into trouble here a couple of times. Let me see if I can pull up any of those incidents."

He typed, and then waited. "We had a volunteer put together an excellent database for us last year, but this computer is so old it takes a while to sort through everything."

"How many computers do you have here?"

"Let's see. Vivek, whom you saw out front, helps with government benefits and paperwork. Barbara works with recovering addicts. And we have a third station for a volunteer who comes in to lead workshops. Plus two computers for visitors to use, though we could use two more."

"And yours," I said. "That's six. I may be able to help you." I explained how Eastern regularly replaced computers, though I didn't know what they did with those they carted away. "I'll have to talk to someone at Eastern first."

"Anything you could do would be welcome." He looked back at his computer. "Here we are. Grantay Delius and three other men got into a fight over a video game, back in early 2011. He and DeAndre Dawson were playing against two other men, and one of the opponents accused Grantay of cheating."

He looked at me.

"DeAndre Dawson," I said. "So there's the connection to Friar Lake. Brother Anselm told DeAndre about us, and went out there with Brother Anselm a few times. How is Brother Anselm?"

"He passed two years ago," Macarius said. "But he was ill when you met him. God chose to take him home."

"Well, I'm sorry for your loss, because I know you cared about him. But I'm glad that he's no longer in pain."

"I live upstairs, as you know, and quite often in the evening I miss the old man, the talks we used to have. He came late to the priesthood, as I did, though he was a soldier first, not an ex-con like me."

"I'm curious. Did he ever say what motivated him to become a priest?"

Macarius sat back in his chair. "It's different for each of us, of course. Some of the brothers I met during my novitiate knew from the time they were boys that they were destined for the church, in some way. They had an awareness of spirituality and a desire for worship."

I petted Rochester as I waited for Macarius to continue.

"Others, like Anselm and me, have a flash of inspiration, as Saul did on the road to Damascus. Brother Anselm was in a forest in Vietnam when he realized he was tired of fighting other men. That he had his own inner demons to combat. He left the Army as soon as he could and went to a Christian detox program. He didn't know that he wanted to become a monk—just that he needed God's help to fight against the drugs that were destroying him."

"Vietnam," I said. "It seems so long ago, and yet I'm sure there are still many veterans of that conflict around us."

He nodded. "There are, though they are in their seventies and eighties now, the ones who survived. I noticed that you used the correct term, by the way. The Vietnam conflict."

"Only the United States Congress can declare war on another

country, and they never did while we were sending advisors and materiel and then soldiers. So we can't call it the Vietnam War."

"That's one of the reasons I enjoy talking with you, Steve," he said. "You're a polymath, like me."

I laughed. "I prefer to think of myself as a jack of all trades, master of none. I know a little bit about a lot of things."

Macarius smiled. "Anselm was more single-minded. Once he was clean, and had accepted the strictures of the church as a way to stay that way, he wanted to spread his own kind of Gospel. He worked at a drug rehab program here on the Lower East Side for years, until he retired and went out to pasture at Our Lady of the Waters."

"Did he like it?" I asked. "It's so different from the city."

"I think he did. He became even more spiritual out there. But when the abbey closed, he asked if he could come here to spend his last years. He was able to be helpful in a small way, and have time for contemplation."

"That's the way we look at the Sabbath in Judaism," I said. "Sometimes I wish there was a pilgrimage route I could take, or a kind of Jewish monastery where I could go to rest and contemplate for longer than just a day." I looked down at Rochester. "But fortunately my furry friend here gives me that restfulness, when I lie on the floor beside him and rub his belly, or scratch behind his ears. That endorphin rush is usually what I need."

We finished our pizza and our drinks, and when Rochester saw there was nothing more coming, he settled on the floor beside me.

"Anything else in your database?" I asked.

Macarius shook his head. "Nothing of use. Only a few dates that Grantay had appointments with Vivek."

"Can you cross-reference those dates to ones when Rahim was here? To confirm that they were here at the same time?"

"Our database isn't that sophisticated. But I can run the same search on Rahim. Take down these dates." He read off a series of six to me, and then turned back to his computer. "And now we wait."

"I have another idea," I said. "At Friar Lake, we run a lot of programs for students, as well as community members. I think it would be great if you could come out one day and do a presentation on what you do here. We've had drug-related incidents on campus, in some cases revealing students who had addiction issues. You might talk about how to help a friend or fellow student you think might be having a problem."

"I'd enjoy that," he said.

"And that might be a reason why I can convince Eastern to donate some computers to the Center," I said.

"Excellent." He looked back at his computer. "Now these dates are not comprehensive, you understand. We don't keep track of folks who drop in to chat with their friends or play a game or two. These are only the dates when people have appointments."

He read the dates when Rahim had been at the Center, and one of them matched with a date when Grantay had been there. I made a note of that.

"I really appreciate this, Macarius," I said.

"You can understand, I'm sure, why I'm more willing to share information with you than with the FBI," he said. "It's important that our clients feel safe coming here."

"I understand. And I know that you want to see justice for whoever killed Rahim."

"That's a funny word," Macarius said. "Sadly, not one we use a lot around here."

Chapter 25

How Many Witnesses?

Rochester and I walked slowly back to the car, so he could continue to sniff all the amazing smells. "Hey, I could write a TV show about a dog in Manhattan," I said to him. "Call it *Scents and the City*. What do you think?"

He lifted his leg against a skinny tree trunk.

Beside us, I heard the screech of brakes and the blat of a horn and looked over just in time to see a bike messenger zoom in front of a Mercedes, and the biker give the driver the finger. I laughed. New York hadn't changed all that much since I'd left.

We skirted a pile of debris that looked too nice to be trash and I realized, from the uniformed men carrying stuff out of a brownstone and the angry young woman behind them, that someone was probably being evicted.

Life was a lot easier in River Bend. I didn't feel like I had to worry about speeding cars when I took Rochester out for his walks. We could stroll down Sarajevo Way at any time of night without fear of criminals with guns or pepper spray. The only graffiti on our streets was spray-painted lines indicating the presence of underground pipes.

Now, if we could only resolve the tree issue, our community could return to that sense of peace and tranquility.

I tugged on Rochester's leash and hurried him toward the car.

I waited until I was out of the city to call Hank Quillian. "Brother Macarius told me several things," I said. "First, that Lafontaine Delius goes by the nickname Grantay, which is Haitian Creole for big. Very muscular guy, very tall."

"That corresponds with the description we have of him."

"Back in 2011, Grantay and his friend DeAndre Dawson were playing a video game at the center against another twosome, and a fight erupted. The fight isn't important, but it proves that DeAndre and Grantay were acquainted."

"Were you a lawyer in some former life?" Hank asked. "Because you frame your arguments like one."

"A computer programmer," I said. "Same idea only with bits and bytes."

He laughed, and I continued.

"Since DeAndre learned about Friar Lake through a brother at the Center, it's possible he would have told Grantay about the property. Once it shut down, it was empty and isolated, and Grantay could have seen it as a good place to hide his loot."

"That's a stretch, but I'll buy it," Hank said.

"And finally Macarius confirmed that at least on one occasion, Grantay and Rahim were at the center at the same time."

"That's interesting, but since they were arrested for the same crime, I already can confirm that they knew each other."

"Oh. Right."

"I appreciate your help, Steve. I had an agent visit the Brotherhood Center the other day, and he got a chilly reception, as you might imagine. Your connection with Macarius has been helpful."

He paused, and for a moment I thought the call had dropped. "What's your impression of Macarius? He's an ex-con himself. And according to records, he only spent the minimum time at a monastery before he moved to New York and set up the Center."

"I like him. We bonded because we both had been in prison, and we both turned our lives around. I think he's a good man trying to do good work. You don't think he's involved in these crimes, do you?"

"I have a suspicious nature. A guy keeps company with bad operators, I start to suspect him. But I don't have any evidence against Macarius. I'm glad to know you have a good opinion of him."

He ended the call, and I continued to Friar Lake, thinking about Macarius. Yeah, he was around ex-cons all the time, many of whom returned to a life of crime despite his best efforts. But I had to believe that there were good people like him in the world.

I didn't have much time to spend at Friar Lake Tuesday afternoon after returning from New York, and I was busy answering emails and telling reporters that they had to speak with Jodie Phillips for any information about Eastern or the stolen goods.

Then Rochester stood up on his hind paws and began sniffing my computer. "There are only bits and bytes in there, not treats," I said.

He plopped back on his butt and stared up at me. "Fine, I'll give you a treat."

I handed him a peanut butter cookie from a plastic bag I kept in my desk, but he didn't want it. He went back up to sniff the computer.

"You're reminding me I promised Macarius I'd see if we can give him any computers," I said. "Good boy." I petted him, and he settled down to munch his cookie as I called Oscar LaVista, Eastern's director of information technology. I'd been on a committee with him in the past, and we'd bonded over shared problems with the computer infrastructure at the college.

"Hey, Oscar. Thanks for helping out with the connectivity problems we had at Friar Lake a couple of weeks ago. The tech you assigned to us really did a great job."

"I'm glad to hear it. Any new problems out at Friar Lake?"

"No problems, but I have a question about what you do with older computers you replace."

"If they're still usable, we wipe the hard drives and donate them to charity," he said.

I explained about the Brotherhood Center, and its connections to Eastern. "Brother Macarius is a great guy and he's doing good work with ancient equipment. I'm hoping to get him out here to give a program, and I'd like to thank him by donating some computers."

"What does he need?"

"He's got four staff members who use computers, and he also has a couple that his clients can use. Anything we can give him would make it easier for his staff and volunteers to access the center's database. And they have regular visitors who don't have online access where they're living and depend on the center's equipment to help them file for benefits and so on."

"Hold on and let me see what we've got."

I heard him typing. "I can give him ten PCs. I'll have them loaded with some basic software. When do you need them?"

"I'll let you know. Thanks."

I looked at my schedule. When could I fit in a program with Macarius? Since we'd cancelled everything that week, I had an opening on Friday—but could we put something together quickly enough? I called one of the staff in the Student Advising Office I knew, a small, birdlike woman named Lori Keats, and told her about Macarius and what the center was doing.

"I wondered if we could present a program about how organizations like the Brotherhood Center are providing help for people with real challenges," I said. "Our students who are interested in psychology and social work might be interested in careers doing what he does."

"We have a number of students interested in sociology who want to get first-hand experience," she said. "We're always looking for organizations that could offer internships, and we have a lot of students who come from the greater New York area. They might be interested in working with him and his group during the summer."

"That's great," I said. "The Brotherhood Center helps a lot of people. Not only ex-cons, but people who are unhoused for a variety of reasons, and people with substance abuse problems."

"That's another connection," Lori said. "Did you know we have a chapter of Al-Anon Family for teens at Eastern? It's open to anyone with an interest, and we have students who've had substance abuse issues as well as those with family members who have a problem. Our next meeting is Friday afternoon. I know it's short notice, but do you think he could speak then?"

"I can ask. How would you feel about having the program out here at Friar Lake? Macarius wants to come out here because of the connections between us and his center, and I have availability then."

"Hold on. Let me see if I can get the van." While she typed, I leaned down and stroked Rochester's head. He looked up at me with a doggy grin.

After a moment, she said, "Yes, I can get hold of the van and bring ten students out there. And many of our members have their own transportation. I think they'd love it."

When I hung up with her, I called Macarius. "I've been looking for a way to get you down here to Friar Lake so you can see the property, but also to talk to our students about the work you're doing at the Brotherhood Center. Do you ever offer internships to college students?"

"We do. We can't afford to pay, but we collaborate with a group that places college students with us and provides them with a stipend. Of course, it's best to get ones who live in the city or the boroughs who can stay with their families during the summer."

"I think we have a real opportunity to connect our students who are interested in psychology and social work with you, to get real on-the-ground experience," I said. I told him about Lori and the work her office was doing. "There's only one problem. She'd like to combine a visit from you with a meeting of their Al-Anon Family club, and that's on Friday afternoon."

"That works out well for me, because we have a rental van this week for some deliveries we need to make, and I can drive down to you Friday afternoon."

"Excellent! I'm glad you're going to have a van, because we may be able to give you some used computer equipment."

"We would appreciate anything you can provide."

I confirmed a few details with him, and then called Oscar, who said that he could bring the computers out to Friar Lake on Friday afternoon to hand over to Macarius.

"Friday's going to be a busy day for us," I said to Rochester. I started ticking things off on my fingers.

"We have to make sure the chapel is ready for the event. I need to order some refreshments from the cafeteria. Lori Keats has to get her kids out here in the van, and Oscar has to have all the computer equipment ready to hand over."

I looked down at him. "Think we can get all that done?"

He woofed once, and I petted his head.

By the end of the day, Joey and the guy from Shakespeare had made real progress on the dais, but they still had to sand and stain some new boards, and then put all the statues back in place. "And then as long as I've got him here, there are a few other things I need help to fix. Nothing drastic, just some long-term maintenance. That way you can charge his time to the renovation budget."

"I like that idea," I said. "When do you think you'll be finished?"

"We can wrap everything up by tomorrow afternoon, and be ready for full operation on Thursday."

"That's great."

I was pleased with the way everything had come through so easily. On my way home I called Rick and filled him in on my trip to New York. Not that anything I'd learned mattered to him professionally, but he was still my friend and sounding board.

When I was finished, I asked, "What's happened to Malgorzata?"

"Arrested and processed. The judge granted her release on her own recognizance, because she explained that she wouldn't be able to post bail. Apparently she mortgaged her house to support her son's business, and she lives on her Social Security."

"Really makes Vic Davis out as a bad guy, doesn't it?" I asked. "Aside from stealing from the HOA where his mother lives. I'll bet he spent that money from her mortgage on that boat of his."

"By the way, Bahamas authorities confirmed that his boat landed in Bimini, which is the closest port to Florida. The state police are still investigating the situation with River Bend, and if they come up with a charge against Davis, they'll have to extradite him."

When I took Rochester out for his evening walk, Bob Freehl was standing with Pete Szabo, who for once wasn't on his three-wheeled bike. Instead he had Malgorzata's white Westie on a leash. The dog yipped angrily at Rochester and we stood back while I asked Pete why he was walking the dog.

"I live next door to her," he said. "I do favors for her, since she's all alone. I take her to the grocery or to pick up prescriptions. She asked me to take Mishu out for a walk because she's so upset."

The dog looked up at him and snarled. I figured Pete would be lucky to finish the walk without getting bitten. In my experience, nice people had nice dogs, and nasty people had dogs that hadn't been trained to behave properly.

"You know she has a son in town, right?"

Pete cocked his head. "She told me that her son has a very demanding job and can't get out here to see her very often. The only vehicle I've seen near her house is the truck from Tree-B-Gone."

"Exactly. That's her son's business. Her name is Malgorzata Debicki Davis Stopnicki, and Vic Davis is her son."

Bob didn't say anything, but he looked uncomfortable.

"She's the secretary of his corporation," I continued. "Which means she has a fiduciary responsibility for that debt. The association could get a lien against her house for the money—except she mortgaged it to the top and gave the money to her son."

"How do you know all this?" Pete demanded.

"You can do an Internet search on any public company," I said.

"If Catalina was doing her job, we'd have known Malgorzata was Vic's mother, and the company was in financial trouble before we signed the contract."

Mishu wouldn't stop yapping at Rochester. My dog barked a warning and the Westie got so frightened he tangled his leash around Pete's legs.

"This whole community has turned against her because of her son," Pete said. "She's had a difficult life. She fled Poland after the war because she was a freedom fighter and they would have put her in prison if they'd caught her. She worked her whole life and then lost her husband. She doesn't deserve to be persecuted the way she has been."

"Bob, you were a cop," I said. "You think Malgorzata will see any prison time for killing Arnold?"

"She didn't kill him," Pete protested. "She hit him with her cane. It's not her fault he fell."

"She hit him, he fell, he's dead," I said.

Pete started to speak again but Bob spoke over him. "I understand they've charged her with involuntary manslaughter," he said. "That means she didn't intend to kill him but her actions resulted in his death. The district attorney will make the decision to prosecute her. He'll have to consider her age and the circumstances."

"There were a dozen witnesses," I said. "A dozen of our neighbors who saw Arnold alive one minute and then dead the next, because of something Malgorzata did. I'll be happy to join any protest at the DA's office to make sure she stands trial."

"How many witnesses were there at your trial?" Pete demanded. "The one where they sent you to prison for two years?"

Bob stared open-mouthed, first at Pete, then at me. Mishu kept yapping.

"My personal situation has no connection here," I said, as my heart rate soared. "I didn't kill anyone. Malgorzata did."

I tugged on Rochester's leash. "Now, if you'll excuse me, I have to finish my dog's walk."

Chapter 26

Blood Pressure

Rochester knew something was wrong, so he did his business quickly and we hurried home. When we got there, my heart was still racing and my hands were shaking.

"What's the matter?" Lili asked when I walked into the kitchen.

"We may have to move." I collapsed onto one of the Windsor-backed wooden chairs. Instead of heading to his water bowl, as he usually did when we came in, Rochester stayed by my side, his head on my knee.

Lili washed her hands, dried them on a dish towel, and came to sit across from me. "What happened?"

I told her about meeting Pete and Bob and Malgorzata's Westie. "The dog kept barking and I was getting really irritated. Pete was trying to minimize what Malgorzata did and I wasn't having it. Even if she didn't mean to, she killed him."

"And why does that lead to us having to move? You think she's coming after you next?"

I shook my head. "Pete Szabo is. For whatever reason, he's been snooping into my past. This evening he confronted me, in front of Bob Freehl, about my trial in California.'"

"That's in your past, Steve. All he can do is spread some nasty rumors about you. But people here in River Bend know you. They'll take your side."

"I think he knows I've been helping Rick in the past," I said. "And he's been challenging me. How do I know anything about Malgorzata?"

"And how do you? You haven't done anything illegal, have you?"

I shook my head. "I haven't. All the records I accessed are public information. But some of the things I've said have come from Rick. For example, Rick called the harbor in Fort Lauderdale and they told him that Vic Davis took his boat out."

"That wasn't privileged information," Lili said. "And it was relevant to what was happening with Tree-B-Gone."

"Still, I think I should go over to Rick's and talk to him. I don't want him to get in trouble for anything I've said or done."

"I was just starting dinner. Why don't you wait until after we eat."

"I can't eat anything now. But let me call Rick. I don't want to interrupt their meal."

I called Rick's cell. "What's up?"

"I'm not disturbing your dinner, am I?"

"Tamsen brought out a beautiful pumpkin pie, but I haven't dug into it yet."

"Can I come over? Twenty minutes or so? Give you time to digest?"

"What's wrong?"

"I need to talk to you. Face to face."

"I don't like the sound of that," he said. "But you come over whenever you want. We'll talk."

I ended the call. "You'd better take Rochester with you," Lili said. "He's already agitated, and if you go out without him he'll fuss at the door until you get home."

I stroked the golden fur along Rochester's back. "You're a sweet boy," I said. "You know that Daddy's upset."

"And he knows that petting a dog can lower your blood pressure," Lili said. "You sit with him for a few minutes before you get behind the wheel."

"Everybody in this house is smart except me," I said. "You're right. I'll sit with him."

"You are a good man, Steve Levitan. You're smart and you're kind and no one can take any of that away from you."

She got up from her chair and kissed me on the cheek. "Now I'm going to fix myself some dinner. There will be leftovers for you if you want."

I sat and watched her cook, stroking Rochester. How did I get so lucky? And why did I keep doing and saying stupid things that jeopardized my life?

After a few minutes my heart rate had slowed but I still felt that hollow place in my stomach. "You want to go see Uncle Rick?" I asked Rochester. "And play with Rascal?"

He jumped up and danced around in a circle. "I'll take that as a yes."

I kissed Lili goodbye and Rochester and I drove over to Rick's house. As soon as we walked up the pavement to the front door, I heard Rascal's barks from inside, and Rochester answered him.

We didn't even have to ring the bell. Rick opened the door and Rochester rushed in, and the two dogs skidded away from us. "Come into my study," Rick said. "I already poured two glasses of brandy."

"I probably shouldn't drink on an empty stomach, but I can manage one," I said, as I followed him. Through a doorway I saw Tamsen and Justin at the kitchen table, and waved at them.

Rick's study was a comfortable room with a couch, a desk and two chairs. I sat on the couch and he pulled a chair up across from me. "What's going on?"

I went back to the beginning of my interactions with Pete Szabo. "It was weird from the start, like he knew things about me," I said. "But I brushed them off. Then this evening I ran into him walking Malgorzata's dog."

I repeated what we had said to each other.

"What an ass," Rick said, after I was finished. "I'll bet he has a few secrets he wouldn't want broadcast around River Bend."

"I'm sure," I said. "But I'm not going to dig. That would only get me in more trouble." I sniffed the brandy and inhaled the rich scent, then took a tiny sip.

"I'm with you there, brother," he said. "But you've reported a threat against you to a police officer, and that gives me the leeway to do some digging on him."

"I don't want to drag you any farther into this than you already are."

He brought his snifter to his lips and sipped, then put it down. "If everything you've said is correct, and I have enough experience with you to believe it's so, then you haven't done anything in this case that could be used against you, or me. In the past, you've stepped over the line a couple of times, and I've ignored it. But unless Pete Szabo has in-depth access to police records there's nothing he can prove."

Rochester and Rascal came rushing in the room, and Rochester's tail was wagging like a metronome at its maximum tempo. He knocked over a copy of Rick and Tamsen's wedding picture, and I hurried to pick it up.

"Sorry about that," I said, as I put it up on a higher shelf.

"Don't worry," he said. "The dog has given me an idea."

He swiveled over to his desk and turned on the computer there. "What are you looking for?" I asked.

"Give me a minute. It might not be anything at all."

Rascal sprawled out beneath Rick's legs, and Rochester sat beside me. I took another sip of brandy and petted him for a minute while Rick typed. "I thought so," he said. "Three months ago, the Register of Wills and Clerk of the Orphans Court in Doylestown issued a marriage license. To Pete Szabo and Malgorzata Stopnicki."

"They're married?" I asked.

He peered at the screen. "The license was issued on January 15, 2011. The couple then has to be married by an officiant, and the license returned to the clerk within ten days. It looks like the license was never returned."

"So they're not married," I said. "But at some point they considered getting married. I wonder what stopped them."

"Hold on," he said. "I have another idea."

"You realize our roles are being reversed here," I said, as he typed. "Usually I'm the one who gets the weird ideas and snoops around."

"Maybe I'm learning from you. Or maybe I've been the trained police detective all along and I've been humoring you."

I laughed. Rochester sensed I was feeling better, and he slumped to the ground by my side.

Rick finished his brandy while waiting for the computer to work its magic. "I did some cross-checking of dates," he said eventually. "Two days after the license was issued, Malgorzata signed off on a mortgage on her house. The appraised value of her property is $400,000, and the mortgage was issued for $380,000."

"Which we think she turned over to her son," I said. "No wonder Pete backed out of the marriage."

Rick did some more clicking. "Pete owns his home outright. So maybe the plan was for her to mortgage her house, move in with him, and rent hers out."

"The HOA has been discussing rules against short-term renters," I said. "If I recall correctly, Pete has been arguing that we should allow them."

Rick turned back to the computer. While I waited for his next revelation, I sipped the brandy. It was hot on my throat but warm by the time it settled in my stomach.

After a moment Rick said, "There's an Airbnb listing at Malgorzata's address, but it's currently not available."

I sat back in my chair. "Maybe because of the way we were raised, and the time, I have this stereotypical idea of elderly people," I said. "My mother's mother was a volunteer for the Red Cross, sewing cotton bandages. Her sister played mahjongg and her brother-in-law played the stock market."

Rick nodded. "Sounds a lot like my grandparents. White-haired, spoiling their grandchildren, contributing to the community."

"But these people are conniving in all kinds of ways," I said. "Fraudulent business activities, high-risk home loans, gambling on the chance to run a short-term rental operation."

He shrugged. "Maybe they were forced into it," he said. "Not enough money for retirement, inflation, medical bills."

"I have nothing to back this up," I said, "but it would not surprise me if Malgorzata lobbied to get her son the contract, knowing he would run off with the money."

"But none of the three of them could count on Malgorzata knocking Arnold Lafoon on his ass and cracking his head open." Rick shook his head. "Or what a can of worms the investigation would open."

I took the last sip of my brandy. "Thanks. I feel a lot better now." I stood up. "Come on, Rochester. Let's see what leftovers Mama Lili has for us."

Chapter 27

Provenance

When we got home, Lili was upstairs. I opened the refrigerator and found a plate of *arroz con pollo* waiting for me. Lili was such an artist at heart—she'd even arranged the two chicken thighs across from each other, surrounded by a mound of rice, peas, and bits of red pimento. My mouth watered just looking at it.

While I reheated it in the microwave, Rochester sat on his butt and stared at me. "Your food is in your bowl," I said. I pointed toward it, but he kept staring at me.

"What? Is there something you need?"

I looked around. He had food in one bowl, clean water in another. From the kitchen, I could see his favorite toys scattered around the living room. "You want attention? Is that it?"

I reached down and scratched beneath his neck, and then the microwave dinged. I carried my plate to the table. Rochester went into the living room and I began to eat. I tried to let everything go, focusing on the smell of the garlic, the way the chicken separated so easily from the bone, the taste of the *sofrito*, or sauteed onion, garlic and red pepper, that made the dish uniquely hers.

Well, it was really her mother's dish, but Lili had learned to cook from watching Senora Weinstock prepare a mixture of food from her Ashkenazi Jewish heritage leavened with that of Cuba, the country that had taken her family in as World War II refugees.

I heard Rochester bumping things around in the living room. "Rochester!" I called. "Don't get into trouble."

He came toward me then, wagging his tail, with a paperback book in his velvety jaws. It was a comfort read for me, one of the Mrs. Pollifax books by Dorothy Gilman. An elderly woman volunteers as a spy for the CIA, and then works as an espionage agent around the world.

I took it carefully from him. "Thank you, boy. Are you saying I need to relax and read something fun?"

He went down on his front paws and looked at the floor. That was usually a "no" response from him.

I looked more closely at the book. In this adventure, she was sent to Thailand to pick up an important piece of information, too valuable to be entrusted in the mail.

"Am I supposed to look for something?" I asked him.

He looked up at me, but that was it.

I was frustrated, and my food was getting cold. I finished eating and then looked at the paperback again. It was over thirty years old and in delicate condition.

Then I had a flash of inspiration. "This reminds me of the missing book from the Belden Museum theft," I said to Rochester. "Is that what you were trying to tell me?"

He jumped up, wagging his tail and yipping.

"I guess that's it," I said. I scratched behind his ears and told him he was a good boy. I washed my dishes and put them in the dishwasher, then moved over to my regular laptop at the dining room table. What did Rochester think I needed to know about that missing book?

According to the *New York Times* article that had mentioned it, the book was "an 18th century diary by the German explorer Carsten

Niebuhr, a member of the Royal Danish Arabia Expedition, which took place from 1761-1767."

I wondered if it was really an important book, or just something that could have gotten lost along the way. I did some Googling and discovered that it was called, not surprisingly, *The Royal Danish Arabia Expedition.*

Niebuhr was the son of a German farmer, educated at home and then at one of Germany's best universities, where a mentor had suggested he join a scientific expedition to Egypt, Arabia, and Syria. Its principal goal was to clarify certain parts of the Old Testament with modern methods of cartography. After he was chosen, he spent a year and a half studying mathematics, cartography, and navigational astronomy so that he could be of service to the expedition.

That was admirable. I couldn't imagine any of the students I'd taught at Eastern—or really, anyone I'd gone to college or graduate school with – going to that length to prepare for something. A modern-day equivalent was training for the Olympics or one of those round-the-world sailing championships.

Perhaps his emphasis on preparation was what enabled him to survive, because one by one, the other members of the expedition succumbed to effects of the climate. The source I read suggested that Niebuhr saved his own life and restored his health by adopting native dress and eating native food.

That was all admirable. But why was his book important? Because it was old?

I read on. "He stayed in Bombay for fourteen months and then returned home by way of Muscat, Bushire, Shiraz and Persepolis." Muscat was in Oman, and I learned that the last three were in Persia, what was today Iran.

The final entry in his biography was what appeared to have made his voyage important. "His copies of the cuneiform inscriptions at Persepolis proved to be a key turning-point in the decipherment of cuneiform, and the birth of Assyriology."

He also "completed 28 town plans of significant historical value because of their uniqueness for that period. In summary, Niebuhr's maps, charts and plans constitute the greatest single addition to the cartography of the region that was produced through field research and published in the 18th century."

Lili came downstairs then. "What are you up to?" she asked.

I told her about my research into the missing book, and its author. "It's really fascinating," I said. "His survival, his mapmaking skills, and what he learned on his travels, are what make the book valuable, as well as its age."

"Are there other copies out there?" she asked.

"I did some hunting on used book sites, and while I found copies of other books Niebuhr wrote, I can't find any copies of *The Royal Danish Arabia Expedition* available in the original printing."

I looked back at the notes I'd taken. "The book was published in six volumes over the span of ten years, finishing in 1778. As far as I can tell, the missing volume is the first of those, dated 1768."

"1768," Lili said. "That's almost 250 years ago. It's amazing that a book can still be here so long after it was printed."

"There are other books from that time for sale online for several thousand dollars." I looked up at her. "If someone wants to sell a painting or an antique, they usually have to list the provenance, don't they?"

She shrugged. "You use provenance to help determine if an item is authentic. If you say your painting is by a 19th century master, can you show the trail of ownership since then? If you can't, then there's a greater possibility that it's a fake. Or that it was stolen."

She sat back in her chair. "Philip collected rare books for a while, so I learned that the most important factors are condition, binding, and completeness. Provenance isn't as important, unless there's something unique in the book's history."

As an inveterate reader, I was intrigued. "Such as?"

"Well, if a book was owned by someone famous, or printed somewhere special, or has a particularly timely value. For example, let's say Karl Marx gave Friedrich Engels an early printing of *Das Kapital*, and Engels marked it up with his own ideas. That would be interesting to collectors because of who they were and because it demonstrates an exchange of ideas."

"Wow."

"At one time, Philip owned a copy of *The Hobbit* that had been inscribed to a man named Gervase Mathew. He was a friend of Tolkien's and occasionally attended meetings of the Inklings. So the signature and the inscription, as well as the relationship between Tolkien and Mathew, made that book more valuable."

"But it doesn't sound like sales receipts or proof of ownership matter that much," I said. "Most of the book descriptions I read didn't indicate who owned them in the past, or who had put them up for sale. So that means that whoever has the copy of this book can list it for sale online without identifying where it came from."

"There are also private book buyers," Lili said. "People who collect a certain kind of book and don't go through regular channels."

"But could whoever broke into the Belden Museum and stole the book have the savvy to sell it?" I asked.

Lili shrugged. "What would it take?"

I thought for a minute. "A smart guy with some computer knowledge could find the description of similar books online and copy that. Then set up a seller account and post the book."

"Could the Belden Museum find that listing?" Lili asked.

"I suppose. But their focus is the artifacts, so they might not even be looking at books for sale. And there might not be anything they could do about it, unless they tagged the item in some way they could identify. Without provenance, it's hard to say something stolen was yours, and not a similar item."

Lili stood up. "I'm making myself a cup of tea before bed. Do you want one?"

"I'll pass, thanks."

I looked back at my screen. It appeared that Grantay Delius was the survivor of the two thieves who had broken into the Belden Museum. Did he have the book? Had he or Rahim already sold it before stashing the rest of the goods at Friar Lake? There was some evidence that they'd tried fencing items back in 2011, after the theft and presumably before storing the rest.

I looked down at Rochester, who was snoozing beside me. I reached down and stroked his golden fur, and he twitched in his sleep. "Good clue, boy," I said. "Now I have to figure out how it matters."

Chapter 28

Crowd Control

Wednesday morning River Bend was very still. No one walking dogs, no trash collections disturbing the quiet, only the occasional sound of a car passing. I was glad. This was the way I loved my neighborhood, and I was sorry that it took the death of an elderly man to shock us back.

At Friar Lake, Joey was continuing the chapel repairs. He was running a polisher over the repaired floor of the dais, and the carpenter from Shakespeare was rebuilding a bookcase that held ancient hymnals.

I put together the paperwork I needed to host Macarius on Friday, and let Joey know. "Our first program after the shutdown," I said. "Seems appropriate that it's Macarius."

"I'm eager to meet him. He sounds like an interesting dude."

"He is." I walked back to my office and called Jodie, and she arranged to send out a press release making it sound like Macarius was the featured speaker at our reopening ceremony.

"I know Kelly Suarez wants to keep milking the story of the stolen articles," she said. "And I'm fine with that. Any positive mention of Eastern in the press is welcome."

Then I called Tony Rinaldi.

"As you know, we've identified Lafontaine Delius as a person of interest in the death of Rahim McCloud," he said. "We have his fingerprints on the broken lock at the front door of your chapel, but until we can interview him and get his story there's nothing else we can do."

"If you'd like to talk to Brother Macarius yourself, he's coming to Friar Lake on Friday," I said.

"That would be interesting."

I gave him the details and sat back. I was eager to have Macarius come out to Friar Lake, because there were so many threads that tied him to us, from the visits by Brother Anselm to the stolen items from the museum to the deaths of DeAndre Dawson and Rahim McCloud. And I liked the guy, and thought he would be able to connect to our students in a different way from our faculty and advisors.

Thinking of DeAndre reminded me of his half-brother, Ka'Tar Winston, and I used the college's e-mail system to let him know that Macarius would be out on Friday, and that he could contact Lori Keats for a ride with her group if he wanted. Finally I called Deana Popescu to follow up with her.

"Hi, Deana, it's Steve Levitan from Friar Lake," I said. "I wanted to follow up with you about the man who died out here earlier this week."

"Yes, I've been thinking about him. I saw the article in the paper this morning. He was one of the men who robbed that museum in New York?"

"That's true. So he really had no connection to Eastern."

"But he died on our property. Would you mind if I came out to the chapel and said a prayer in his memory?"

"That would be lovely." I told her about the program we had planned with Macarius on Friday. "Would you like to join us? Macarius knew Rahim briefly in New York."

"I'd like that." I gave her the information.

It was great to get back to ordinary rhythms at Friar Lake after all the uproar. I spent the rest of the day planning for the remainder of the spring semester, and taking a couple of long walks with Rochester through the blossoming trees.

But all that calm was destroyed when I got back to River Bend. I couldn't turn onto Bucharest Place, as I normally would have to access Sarajevo Way, because there were cars parked on both sides of the street. Halfway down the street I saw a crowd of people.

I detoured around so that I could get to my driveway, then grabbed Rochester and his leash to walk over to where I'd seen the disturbance.

Bob Freehl was standing at the back of a small crowd in what I recognized as his retired police stance. "What's going on?" I asked.

"See the truck in the driveway over there?"

"Tree-B-Gone," I said. "Did the company finally send someone to do the work?"

He shook his head. "That's Malgorzata's house. People think her son has come back from the Bahamas and they want to talk to him."

Up at the front of the crowd I saw Jennifer Dodge, chair of the tree committee, with a couple of my fellow members. "I'm going to back up Jennifer," I said.

"I'm staying back here in case there's trouble," he said. "I've got 911 on speed dial."

The crowd was a mix of older, retired neighbors and stay-at-home moms, though I expected they'd have to get home to fix dinner, perhaps to be replaced by spouses returning from work. I moved easily through the crowd, who were all talking about Tree-B-Gone and how it should be held accountable.

I walked to the edge of the crowd and called Rick. "Another gathering at River Bend," I said. "This time people think Vic Davis has come back and he's in his mother's house."

"Your neighborhood is driving me nuts," he said. "I'll get a couple of officers out there in case there's trouble."

Rochester and I moved through the crowd toward Jennifer,

though it wasn't easy because so many people wanted us to stop so they could pet Rochester and tell me how good-looking he was.

I reached Jennifer as the front door opened, and Vic Davis stepped out, with his giant schnauzer on a leash. I was pleased that he'd gotten the dog back.

"I want to apologize to all of you," Vic said.

"You should!" Mary Kate Donahue yelled.

"I had some business difficulties and I let them get out of hand," Vic continued. "And then I got scared and I ran away. I shouldn't have done that."

"No, you shouldn't have," Mary Kate said.

"Let him speak," a young mother said to Mary Kate. She had an infant strapped to her chest in a brown contraption with a bear's head.

"I've been talking with my mother, who is a valued member of your community."

"And a murderer!"

I didn't know the name of that elderly man, but I imagined he must have been a friend of Arnold Lafoon.

The crowd wasn't making it any easier for Vic. He was swallowing hard and his body was shaking.

I stepped up. "All right, let's everybody calm down and give Mr. Davis the chance to speak. This has been a very difficult time for all of us, but we owe him the chance to make things right."

He looked at me and nodded. "Thank you. I am meeting with the bank tomorrow morning with my mother and a friend of hers, who has agreed to provide me with some operating capital. I promise to have a crew back here as soon as possible to do the work you have already paid me for."

He took a deep breath. "I hope you will give me that opportunity. And once I have finished removing the trees in the first phase of River Bend, I hope you will be satisfied with my work and allow me to work out the rest of the contract."

I looked at Jennifer.

"Thank you, Mr. Davis," she said. "The tree committee will work with you to expedite the removal and replacement of the trees in phase one." She turned to the crowd. "And as always, the work of any committee of residents will be open and transparent to all residents."

Henry Meskin appeared from the side of the crowd, where he'd been keeping his head down. "Thank you, Jennifer. Now we all know what sadly happened the last time we had an angry crowd here in River Bend. Please, return to your homes and trust your board of directors and the management company to continue to deal with this problem."

People began dispersing, and Vic Davis went back inside his mother's house. "I wonder what made him come back?" Jennifer asked, as Henry joined us.

Henry leaned down to pet Rochester. When he stood, he said, "Pete Szabo tracked him down in the Bahamas and told him that his mother had been arrested. Vic may be a lousy businessman but he's a good son."

"I hope he can get that loan," Jennifer said.

"I bet it's coming from Pete Szabo," I said. "You know he and Malgorzata were supposed to be married back in January. But I bet that Pete saw what a mess Vic was and called it off."

"I have two kids under ten, and my mother is showing signs of dementia," Jennifer said. Rochester leaned into her and she smiled down at him. "I know how hard it is to look after an elderly parent."

"And you're a good daughter," Henry said.

Jennifer smiled and thanked him, and the three of us went our separate ways, with Rochester stopping periodically to anoint the neighborhood bushes. When I got home, I saw Rick's truck parked next to mine in the driveway. Rick was leaning against it and welcomed Rochester, as I let the golden off his leash and he romped forward.

"I was at the back of the crowd and I saw how you calmed them," Rick said. "Good work."

"The neighbors are basically good people," I said. "You just can't let them get into a mob mentality."

"Amen to that. But I still have to put together a case for the district attorney against Malgorzata. Then he can decide if he wants to prosecute her."

"Will having her son here make a difference?"

"I think so. Even though she's unpleasant, she's still an old woman with health conditions. She could get probation in lieu of incarceration, especially if her son's going to live with her."

"Or her husband," I said. "Maybe Malgorzata and Pete will follow up with that marriage license they took out in January."

"You're never too old to get some nookie," he said. "Good news for the both of us."

"We're hardly as old as they are," I said. "You want to come inside for a drink or something?"

"Nah, I've got to head home. But I'll talk to you soon."

Rochester and I went inside and Rick drove off. Lili got home a few minutes later and I told her about all the fuss she'd missed.

"I'm glad. I want this neighborhood to get back to the peace and quiet we used to have."

"Me, too."

"Did you see Pete Szabo in the crowd?" she asked.

"No. I have a feeling he was inside with Malgorzata."

"Do you think he's going to make trouble for you?"

"I hope not. I bet he's got his hands full with Malgorzata and her son."

Rochester woofed. "Yes, you're my son," I said. "How about dinner?"

He woofed again.

Chapter 29

Security

I felt more secure taking Rochester for a walk on Thursday morning, not worrying about being buttonholed by angry neighbors. I hoped that Pete Szabo was so caught up in dealing with Malgorzata and her son that he wouldn't follow through on his threats to tell the neighborhood about my criminal record.

But if he did, I'd deal with it. I had navigated a year in prison without getting shanked, and since then faced down criminals in the pursuit of justice. I wasn't going to let a cranky old man hurt me or anyone I cared about.

I saw the first robin of spring that day, and noticed new buds on the magnolia at the end of Sarajevo Way. I wondered, not for the first time, why our streets couldn't have normal names. A development outside Yardley took its street names from local colleges and universities; I had a high school friend who lived at the corner of Lehigh and Lafayette. Another was called Westover, and the streets spelled out that word name, beginning with the W and ending with Eton and Radcliffe Roads. Near New Hope, the roads were named for Revolutionary War generals: Greene, Knox, and Wayne—though they'd skipped naming one for Benedict Arnold.

As we rambled, I wondered how I'd have named the streets in River Bend if I'd been given the chance. Delaware, for sure. Then maybe river-related words like channel, island, waterway, tributary? They had to be better than Sarajevo Way and Bucharest Place.

But I'd eventually learned that the guy who secured the development rights to the land was from Eastern Europe, and he wanted to memorialize the world he had left behind.

Fair enough, though I wanted the places and events I'd left behind to stay securely in my memory. I wouldn't want to be reminded of Trial Place, Judgment Lane, Prison Terrace or Miscarriage Way. They were inside me anyway, prone to pop up at any time.

Signs of spring were all around us as Rochester and I drove up River Road. Migrating Canada geese honked from the river and took off in chevrons. The air was fresh when I rolled down the windows, and a whiff of fragrance flew past us as I spotted the pink blossoms of cherry and apple trees. I felt rejuvenated. We'd solved the mystery of the stolen artifacts and drawn Vic Davis back to River Bend to carry out his contract.

Then we spotted a flattened frog in the middle of the road, and I remembered that two people had died— Arnold Lafoon and Rahim McCloud. But they were not my responsibility, I reminded myself. Arnold was an elderly man in poor health, who'd already suffered falls before his fatal one. Malgorzata would have to take responsibility for what she had done to knock him down.

I felt more responsible for Rahim McCloud, because he'd been killed at Friar Lake. It wasn't my job to pursue his killer and bring that individual to justice, but I did feel a connection to him because he'd lost his life at the property I was responsible for. I was glad that Deana Popescu had pressed the issue of saying a memorial prayer for him, which we'd manage after Brother Macarius's talk that afternoon.

I looked over and noticed that Rochester was pawing the seat belt behind him. The safest place in the car for him was on the back seat, using a harness to tether him to the seat belt, but I knew he'd never stand for that. He had to be by my side whenever possible.

But he'd never been bothered by the front seat belt before. "What are you doing, puppy?" I asked, as I turned to drive up the hill. "Is that in your way?"

He looked at me. That meant I wasn't seeing something I was supposed to.

"Seat belt," I said out loud. "Safety? Security? Something here at Friar Lake?"

I pulled up in front of my office and let Rochester out of the car. He rushed over to Joey, who was coming out of the chapel.

"Security," I said again. "Right."

I waved Joey over as Rochester rushed over and jumped up on his legs. "Rochester reminded me of something," I said. "If we'd had better security, could we have prevented Rahim McCloud's death?"

"Better in what way?"

I stood there in the spring breeze as Joey petted Rochester.

"Suppose we had more sophisticated security cameras, which might have alerted me, or the police, when the chapel door lock was broken. Would that have drawn the police out before what went down between Rahim and his killer?"

"Steve. Friar Lake is in the middle of rural countryside. We had no way to expect a New York City criminal to invade our property and end up dead."

"I know. I keep thinking of all the security measures they have in the city. At the Brotherhood Center they have a roll-down grate and a heavy-duty lock on the door."

"But that shouldn't be necessary around us," Joey said.

Rochester wandered off to sniff the edge of a light pole—one that held a security camera. "That's why people come to the country," I said. "To be safer than they are in the city. When I was growing up, we were one of the only families that locked our front door, because my parents had come out from Trenton."

"My parents didn't lock our doors because my brothers and I were always going in and out, or having kids come over to play."

"But you lock your door now in River Bend, don't you?" I asked.

"Yeah, but that's mostly because Mark is careful to lock up the antique store. And we have some of his bigger inventory in our garage."

Rochester returned to my side after anointing the security pole. "It's frightening, the way that crime had been creeping out here, where people have felt safe in the past," I said. "There are marijuana grow houses in Bucks County. Last year a street gang from Trenton crossed the bridge and dumped a body in Morrisville. And Lili has heard about purse snatchers in Leighville, hanging around gyms and cafes."

"If you want, I can look into expanding our security network," Joey said. "I could see us with a few more cameras, and maybe we can tie into the college system so Campus Safety is alerted if anything happens out here. They monitor twenty-four-seven, so they can call the cops."

"That would be great. I'm sure I can convince President Babson to authorize the expense, after what's happened."

"I'll get onto it once I have everything cleaned up," he said. "I have some more small repairs to handle around the property, and we want everything cleaned up and ready for our first visitors tomorrow."

"Let me know how I can help."

Late that morning, Oscar LaVista sent over a tech in a van with ten computers, monitors, keyboards and mice. All that equipment was going to help the Brotherhood Center a great deal with their mission. I helped them unload it and stow it in the far classroom, which backed up against the road that circled the property. That would be an easy place for Macarius to get access to it all.

In the early afternoon Bobby Flett, the current Director of Facilities, pulled into the parking lot. He was nominally our boss, but he rarely left his office at Eastern because he was a very big guy and had difficulty walking. Rochester and I walked to greet him, and I held the dog back until Bobby had extricated himself from the driver's seat of his van.

Bobby was only about five-ten, but every part of him was big. He could have tried out for one of those reality shows about heavily obese people. Because Joey communicated regularly with Bobby's staff, he had told me that he had some kind of problem with his thyroid, and was going into Philadelphia regularly for treatment.

Joey rolled up in a golf cart as I said hello to Bobby. "What brings you out here today?"

Even though it was a cool day, Bobby was sweating heavily, and his voice was raspy. "Heard about the problems you had and wanted to see if I can offer any help." He nodded toward Joey. "This one seems to think he can manage everything on his own. And he generally can, but I want to remind you now and then that our office is available."

"That's good of you," I said. Joey and I helped Bobby into the front seat so Joey could give him a tour. I watched as the golf cart turned around and headed down one of the stone paths. Rochester suddenly began racing toward the trees, and I took off after him.

I realized as we got close to the tree line that he'd spotted a pair of squirrels who were daring enough to encroach on Rochester's turf. The little furry rodents turned tail and rushed for a tree as my dog approached.

The squirrels chased each other around the tree, climbing as they circled it, and I recognized that it must be mating behavior. Well, it was spring after all.

Rochester sat at the base of the tree and watched the two squirrels chase each other. When the female reached the highest branches, she jumped out and the branch bounced beneath her. One more hop and she was on a nearby branch. The male followed her a moment later.

Rochester realized he wasn't going to catch them. He opened his mouth in a big doggy grin and raced back toward the gatehouse, but this time I followed him more slowly.

I kept an eye out for the golf cart and went outside to see Bobby when they returned. "You've done a good job to get everything back up to speed, but you still need some help with polish," he said, the wheeze still in his voice. "I'll send out a pair of housekeepers to dust and vacuum tomorrow morning."

"Thanks, Bobby. That would be great."

I helped him get out of the golf cart and Joey and I watched as he walked to his car. "Poor guy," I said, as Bobby drove away. "You never know what's going on with someone when you only see them from the outside."

As I was walking Rochester back to my office, he had a long trail of drool coming out of his mouth, and when he shook his head violently the string flung up and wrapped itself around his muzzle. "Rochester," I said. I pulled a tissue from my pocket and wiped it up.

I helped Joey do some tidying up, and by the end of the day I was satisfied that things were coming back to normal.

Thursday evening, I saw several neighbors as Rochester and I were walking, and no one complained or yelled. We deliberately didn't go past Bucharest Place and Malgorzata's house.

Over dinner, I asked Lili if she wanted to come over to Friar Lake the following afternoon to see Macarius's presentation. "I wish I could, but I have a grant request for the gallery that I need to finish," she said. "Otherwise I'll have to work on it over the weekend and I'd rather not do that. But send him my love."

"I will. I'm curious to see how our students react to him."

"You mean the outfit? The big monk's robe?"

"Well, that, and the very real-world situation he deals with. College in general is a very insular situation, especially for a school like Eastern. If they were at NYU or Columbia, they'd encounter homeless people, drug deals, street violence. But in Leighville they're sheltered from all that."

"I've seen homeless people in Leighville," Lili said. "And we had that drug scandal last year."

"I know. But it's easier to avoid those situations out in the country. I remember when I was at Eastern, I hardly left campus my whole freshman year. My routine was dorm, classrooms, dining hall, and library. And my parents supported that idea—that I'd been sent away to focus on my education. It wasn't until senior year that I started to think about what I was going to do after I left."

"Did you always want to be an English professor?"

I shook my head. "Not at all. But by the time I started thinking about careers, I was too entrenched in the English major to consider changing. Lucas Roosevelt wasn't the department chair then, he was one of my professors, but one day I sat down with him and asked him if I should go to law school. That's what my parents wanted, and I knew other English majors who were applying."

"What did he say?"

"He quizzed me about what I wanted from life. What I was good at, what I thought I could make money at. I took an editing course that year, and I liked it, and I told him I might want to work in publishing."

"What did he say?"

"He asked me how good I was at typing and filing, because the entry level jobs in publishing in New York were all secretarial for the first few years. And the pay was lousy, so I'd have to live somewhere crummy and depend on my parents for handouts."

"Ouch. Though I'd say that's still a fair assessment."

"Yeah. Then I asked about freelance writing and technical writing. Could I make a living at that? That's when he suggested I go to grad school. He suggested Columbia for journalism, and I liked the idea of moving to the city. I applied to the MA program in English at the same time, and I got in there, but not to the journalism school."

"So that's why you went to Columbia?"

I nodded. "I couldn't see staying in school long enough for a PhD, but Columbia had a free-standing MA program for people who didn't want the doctorate. I found out I could take a few journalism courses as part of my MA. I stumbled into teaching after I graduated, and used some adjunct courses to supplement freelance writing."

"When I started the MFA in photography at the Photo Arts Conservancy, I didn't think I wanted to teach either. I wanted to have the degree as a credential to get photography jobs. But then I started dating Philip and I was doing very ordinary shoots in the city and I wanted something more, so I started taking more classes to keep my brain working."

She sat back from the table. "And then I got divorced and was offered some more interesting work, and I made London my base for a while. The University of London had a PhD program in creative arts—everything from perfumery to puppetry, as we used to say. So I registered there, and they took all the credits I had and let me focus on fieldwork."

"It's funny, we've never really discussed what you did to get your PhD."

"There were some technical classes on how to use different kinds of cameras, and of course Photoshop had come out a few years before so we were learning how to manipulate images. That ended up being the focus of my thesis. I used photos that I took of the Zapatistas in Chiapas and demonstrated how by adjusting the field of vision, determining what went into focus and what was blurred, and so on—how all that contributed to the effect you wanted the photograph to achieve."

She stood up and started clearing the table. "I had a much more doctrinaire, political stance back then. I was more interested in the effects of war on the local people than on taking pictures of the soldiers and the fighting."

"I've noticed that when you take pictures of people today, you're really interested in telling a story, not just creating a beautiful image."

Rochester was underfoot, so I had to skirt around him to put things back in the refrigerator.

"I think of photography as a form of storytelling rather than simply image creation," she said. "That's what I try and teach my students. I ended up taking the department chair position at Eastern because I could have a full-time job with security and benefits, and teach a class every term, and work in a creative environment."

"And it was my good fortune that you did," I said. "Which reminds me. What are we going to do about photography for the wedding. Do you have someone you want to hire?"

"I've been thinking. I have a really talented student who's graduating this spring who wants to make a career out of photography. She's torn between looking for journalism jobs or doing freelance work. I've told her that neither are very secure and she should try to combine both."

"Where's she from?"

"Leighville. She's already sold a few photographs to the local paper, so I suggested she might stick around for a year, live with her folks and polish her skills. She has already agreed to photograph a cousin's wedding in May and a high school friend's in June."

"I think it's sweet to support a student, but do you think we'll get decent photographs? For my bar mitzvah my parents hired a kid who worked at my uncle's drugstore, and half the time he left the lens cap on when he was taking pictures. He never stopped to tell me to comb my hair and the few photos we got were a mess."

"I trust this student. Remember, I've seen her work already. And she'll have some weddings under her belt by October."

I counted the time to October on my fingers. "Seven months," I said. "It seems like a long time now but I'm sure it'll zoom past. It seems like just the other day we were celebrating New Year's Eve at Gracious's house."

"Are you going to ask her to be your matron of honor?" I asked.

"I thought about it. But I think I'd like to ask Tamsen instead. You're going to ask Rick to be your best man, aren't you?"

"I am. Though I thought about Tor, too."

"We don't have to be completely traditional," she said. "Gracious has been telling me about Botswana traditions, and they declare their intentions to the public twenty-one days before the wedding. She's offered to throw us that party at their house. So that would be a way to involve her in the plans."

"Do you think maybe we could invite Tor and Sherri to co-sponsor that party?"

"I think that would be lovely. To demonstrate that both the bride's and the groom's communities approve."

"Rochester and I saw something funny today at Friar Lake," I said. "A squirrel mating dance. One was chasing the other around the trunk of a tree and Rochester was fascinated."

"Fortunately you don't have to chase me around a tree," Lili said. "All you have to do is ask."

I asked.

Chapter 30

Presentation

Friday morning dawned crisp and clear. Bob Freehl was out in his yard planting clusters of purple and blue pansies and johnny jump-ups and I had to rein Rochester in to keep him from anointing them.

"Any news about when they're going to start tree removal?" Bob asked.

"Haven't heard anything yet. The good thing about Vic Davis running off with our money is that it brought the community together. Now most people are resolved to get trees taken out," I said. "And we have a plan for new trees. Three different varieties that don't have invasive root systems. So we'll have trees of varying heights, with different blossoms and a range of fall colors. The end result is going to be better for everyone."

"What did Pete mean when he talked about your trial?" Bob asked.

"I got into some computer trouble in California," I said. "But nobody was injured in any way, and I served my time. Came back here to put it all behind me."

"Interesting that you spend so much time with Rick Stemper,"

Bob said. "He's a good guy, so if he vouches for you, then you're all right in my book."

"Thanks, Bob." Rochester pulled me along, in search of a new smell, and we continued our walk without further incident.

I arrived at Friar Lake at nine, and the ground crew which came out once a week from the college was already at work, sweeping the sidewalks and hosing down the parking lot. Joey and I spent an hour, with Rochester by my side, inspecting the whole property to make sure we were ready to receive visitors.

Then we waited. I processed the invoice from Shakespeare, answered a bunch of emails, and kept looking out the window to make sure I greeted anyone who showed up.

I had invited Macarius to arrive early for his two o'clock presentation. I'd had the cafeteria staff at Eastern prepare a platter of sandwiches, chips and sodas for us, which were laid out in the cafeteria. Shortly before noon, I noticed a white van chugging up the hill, and Rochester and I went outside.

Macarius was wearing his regular brown robe and white socks with leather sandals. Rochester was eager to greet him, jumping around him like a demented kangaroo. "He must remember the pizza crust we shared the last time I saw you," Macarius said.

"Possibly. And he's also an excellent judge of character."

Joey came up to us, and I introduced them. "I'm going to take Macarius down to the lake," I said. "You want to come with us?"

He agreed, and the three of us threaded our way down a set of stairs embedded in the hillside to the single-story house where the abbey's domestic staff had lived. Rochester went ahead of us, daintily picking his way down the steps. When he reached the bottom he raced over to the side of the building, then sat there to wait for us.

"This is where we found DeAndre's body," I said, as we approached the dog.

Macarius crossed himself, then looked around. "Very peaceful," he said. "I hope his soul is at rest. He was a good man, just driven by too many bad influences."

"He did a great job with Ka'Tar," I said. "He'll be here later to hear your presentation."

Macarius beamed. "Yes, DeAndre was a good brother to him."

We strolled around the lakefront for a few minutes. The water was so calm I saw a clear reflection of the chapel in it. A few ducks waddled around the far edge of the water, and I had to call Rochester back to keep him from chasing them.

Eventually we climbed back up to the compound. "I have a surprise for you," I said. "Could you give Joey the keys to your van and come with me?"

"I'm curious," he said, as he handed the keys over.

We walked through the center of Friar Lake to the rear classroom and Joey pulled the van up there. I led Macarius inside, and turned on the lights.

"All these are for you," I said. "Joey and I will help you load them into your van."

Macarius stared at the row of computers and peripherals open-mouthed. "This is more generous than I could have imagined," he said. "Truly, the Savior works in mysterious ways."

"There's a box of manuals over there, if you need them, and a bunch of set-up disks. It'll take you a while to get everything installed, but it should be a lot better than what you have."

He reached out and clasped my hand in both of his. "Thank you, Steve. And please extend my thanks to whoever made this possible."

"You'll meet the college president later," I said. "For now, let's get all this stuff into your van."

The three of us carried boxes outside, and Joey demonstrated his usual genius at spatial organization to get everything carefully loaded. Rochester supervised.

Then Joey and I gave Macarius a brief tour of the rest of the property, ending at the former refectory, where we sat down to lunch.

"I appreciate the way you've kept the spiritual character of the property while updating it," Macarius said. "Do you think I could organize an outing here sometime this summer for our clients? I'm sure it's lovely here when it's hot in the city."

"I'd say we're continuing a long tradition of connection between the Brotherhood Center and Our Lady of the Waters, now Friar Lake," I said. "Though we will have to emphasize that the property is now under surveillance twenty-four-seven, so it's no longer a good place to stash loot."

"Of course," Macarius said with a laugh.

I fed Rochester bits of my roast beef sandwich, and he got some nibbles from Joey and Macarius as well. By the end of our meal he was lolling, fat and happy, on the stone floor.

He still jumped up as soon as we walked over to the chapel. Joey was inside with Macarius getting the projector set up when Babson arrived. He petted Rochester's head and my golden looked up adoringly at him.

"Everything looks even better than before," Babson said, as he looked around. "You know this project is very special to me, Steve. It represents a way for Eastern to grow beyond the physical boundaries of the campus, and to reach out to the local community, and the scholarly one."

As we walked toward the chapel, I told him that Brother Macarius wanted to bring some of his clients out during the summer, and he readily agreed. I really was very lucky to have him as a boss.

I led him inside and introduced him to Macarius, and then Rochester and I went back outside to greet Lori Keats and the van of students. The students were all excited to get away from the confines of the campus, and they were eager to pet Rochester, too.

Ka'Tar was the last one out. "I have bittersweet memories of this place," he said. "Coming here for the Eastern Connection that time in the summer was so great for me, and really showed me that I could fit into college. But then I think of DeAndre and everything he did to get me here."

Rochester nuzzled against one side, and I put my arm around Ka'Tar's shoulders. "That's life, pal. A collection of good and bad memories. I'm very glad that DeAndre was able to be there for you when he was, and get you set on a good path."

A woman I recognized as Deana Popescu arrived in her own car, and then a couple of professors arrived with a motley crew of students. We all filed into the chapel, and the acoustics of the old building were excellent as President Babson gave a brief introduction to Friar Lake and his hopes for it.

Then I stepped up to the podium. "I met Brother Macarius four years ago, and I was impressed with the work that he and the Brotherhood Center do to help those who are down on their luck. I graduated from Eastern College a long time ago, without a very clear picture of what my future would hold. But I was confident, as you all should be, that Eastern provides you with a good foundation for any endeavor."

I paused to clear my throat. "My path was rocky for a while, and while I hope all of you will have a smoother way ahead of you, you may see some trouble. Statistics show that many of you may face addiction to drugs, emotional and psychological difficulties, marital problems, career setbacks, and even a run-in with the law. What President Babson and I hope is that your time here at Eastern will equip you to face those problems head-on. And Brother Macarius is here to demonstrate that help is available to you and those like you, even in the darkest of days."

There was applause, and I turned the podium over to Macarius. Joey dimmed the lights and Macarius began his presentation.

Rochester was sitting beside me in the front row when he began to get restless. "That's a good boy," I said, petting him. I grabbed hold of his collar because I didn't want him running off in the darkness, perhaps scaring one of the students.

Then a tall, bulky figure emerged from the shadows, climbing the newly-installed steps to the dais. He had a gun in his right hand, trained on Macarius.

"I want that book!" he demanded.

Chapter 31

Royal Danish Arabia Expedition

Macarius was the picture of calm as he turned to the man. "I'm afraid I don't know what book you're referring to."

Joey made his way to the electrical panel and flipped the lights on, and it took a moment for everyone's eyes to get accustomed.

"Grantay, isn't it?" Macarius said, in that same calm tone.

I transferred Rochester's leash to Babson, on the dog's other side, and pulled out my cell phone. As Macarius negotiated with Grantay, I texted Tony Rinaldi what was going on and asked him to send uniforms.

"Why don't you put the gun down and let these young people leave the chapel, and then you and I will look around for the book you want," Macarius said.

Because I was close enough to see Grantay's movements, I could tell that he was hyped up on something. The hand holding the gun shook, and he licked his lips frequently, a sign of dry mouth.

"Rahim must have given it to you to hold," Grantay insisted. "Or he told you where he stowed it here."

"This is my first time here at Our Lady of the Waters," Macarius said. "But you've been here before?"

"Don't play stupid with me, old man," Grantay said. Out of the corner of my eye, I saw Lori Keats begin shepherding students out of the chapel. "You know I was here, with Rahim. DeAndre told me this place was abandoned and Rahim and I needed a place to store all that old pottery shit while we waited for the market to cool. We weren't even going to be able to sell most of it, just a couple of the gold pieces to get melted down."

He shook his head. "Stupid of both of us."

"You stored the pieces here, and then the FBI found them," Macarius said.

On the other side of the chapel, I saw the faculty members moving their students outside as well.

"But they didn't find the book!" Grantay said. "I read it in the paper. I know a guy who said he would buy it. Hand it over!"

Rochester was pulling so hard that Babson was having trouble controlling him. I took the dog's leash and we walked quietly up the aisle beside the wall. I wanted to get him outside, but he wouldn't go out the front door. Instead he tugged me ahead, to the aisle along the farther wall.

"I'm afraid I don't have any connection with the FBI," Macarius said. He smiled. "They're not likely to trust me. I was in prison myself, you know."

"I know all about you, old man. You're a waste of time, trying to keep guys from going back to prison. Football and video games and pizza. Ain't gonna solve my problems."

"You know we offer more than that," Macarius said. "Counseling, job placement, housing. We could help you, when you come back from prison."

I was sweating heavily and my hands were wet. As we approached the front of the chapel, Rochester tugged hard against me and my hand slipped through the leash. Before I could call him, he lunged up the steps and launched himself at Grantay.

My heart began to race as the big man stumbled, feeling ninety pounds of golden retriever at his back. I stood there in shock as Macarius jumped forward and grabbed the gun from Grantay's hand.

"On the ground!" Macarius barked, in a completely different tone than the one he'd been using.

Grantay went down on the wooden dais, and Rochester plopped his butt on Grantay's legs. "Good boy," Macarius said, and I assume he was talking to Rochester.

My heart kept racing as I realized what had happened. My dog had done it again, flung himself into danger to protect those he cared about. I loved him for it, but I was also so angry. What if he'd been hurt? He was my precious boy.

Then the rear door flung open, and someone shouted, "Police! Freeze!"

Macarius knelt to the floor and placed the gun there, then kicked it to the side. He stood up with his hands in the air.

Tony Rinaldi stepped into the doorway like a Western sheriff, his right hand on the gun at his hip. Two officers streamed in behind him, weapons raised and aimed at the two men on the dais.

I hurried over to Tony and explained the situation to him, while his officers guarded Grantay and Macarius. "The friar in the robe is our guest speaker, Brother Macarius from the Brotherhood Center in New York. I believe the man on the floor is Grantay Delius."

"You can let the brother go," Rinaldi directed the officer by Macarius. "I mean the friar."

He and I both laughed, more a release of tension than a recognition of his linguistic confusion. An officer leaned down to cuff Grantay's hands behind his back. "Rochester, come to me," I called, and the dog stood up, his front paws on the small of Grantay's back, and opened his mouth wide in a toothy grin. Then he gracefully jumped off onto the wooden floor.

As Rochester made his way down the steps to me, the officers helped Grantay stand up. Rochester came over to me and I knelt down beside him. "You're a good boy," I said into his fur. "Sometimes you take too many risks, but you're a good boy."

I stood up and wiped a tear from my eye. Rochester leaned against my leg and I let one hand rest on his head.

Up on the dais, Tony said, "Lafontaine Delius, you are under arrest for the murder of Rahim McCloud," and then read him his Miranda rights. Any prosecution for the theft from the Belden Museum would come from the Feds, but murder took priority.

The officers led Grantay away, and Tony came over to me. "Thanks for your text," he said. "The students were pretty active, too. We got at least ten 911 calls about a man with a gun out at Friar Lake."

"I imagine we'll see Kelly Suarez out here any minute," I said.

"You can direct her to my office," Tony said. "We'll have an official statement for the press in a short time."

He left in his car, following the officers who had Grantay in custody, and I went over to Macarius. "If our audience is still here, do you feel up to continuing your presentation?"

He wiggled his fingers. "I feel very energized."

I did, too. My fear for Rochester's safety had abided, and it felt like we'd all come through a very difficult time, safely.

I went outside and explained to Lori and the faculty members that it was safe to come back in. "Do you think the students will be too upset to continue?" I asked.

"I'll see." She went over to the two faculty members and spoke with them, and then the three of them addressed the crowd. "Brother Macarius is ready to continue his presentation," Lori said. "If anyone is uncomfortable about going back into the chapel, Ms. Popescu and I will be happy to go over into one of the classrooms with you and talk about what's happened and how you feel about it."

"I feel grateful for Brother Macarius," one boy said,

"And the dog," a girl added, and there was laughter and applause. The two professors led the students inside, and many of them wanted to stop and pet Rochester on the way, telling him what a good boy he was.

"Can I give him a cookie?" a boy asked. "It's chocolate chip."

"Dogs aren't supposed to have chocolate," I said. "But he's a big enough boy to handle a little bit."

The boy gave Rochester the cookie, which he wolfed down.

Lori and Deana stayed outside until the last of the young people had walked in. "I guess no one was that upset," Lori said. "But these are students who are interested in social justice so I think they're more accustomed to seeing the police. And this was a really good demonstration for them of how it's appropriate for law enforcement to behave."

"I'm glad it worked out for all of us."

Rochester and I followed Lori and Deana inside, and Macarius resumed his presentation. While he spoke, Joey set up a couple of tables outside with the extra sandwiches and several plates of cookies, along with a case of bottled water.

When Macarius finished, he received a standing ovation, though I had a feeling that was more for his performance with Grantay than anything else.

Then Deana took the podium and offered a brief prayer in memory of Rahim McCloud, who had been taken from this world too soon.

The students filed outside for their refreshments, and Babson, Rochester and I walked over to Macarius as he was clearing up his notes. "You're a man of many talents," Babson said to him. "I'm glad that Eastern is going to continue our association with the Brotherhood Center."

"I'm very grateful for your support," Macarius said. "Thank you for the computers as well. They'll really make a difference in the work we do for our clients, and we'll be able to provide more computers for those who don't have or can't afford Internet access. You're opening the world to them."

He and Babson shook hands. Then Macarius picked up his folder and the three of us walked toward the front entrance. As we approached, we passed the bookshelf that Joey and the guy from Shakespeare had rebuilt, and Rochester stopped right in front of us, his nose toward the bookcase.

Macarius stopped to pick up one of the books. "This is not what Grantay was looking for, but it is very old," he said. "*The Book of Daily Hours*. I remember using this kind of book when I was a novitiate." He looked at the front pages. "My goodness. This has an 1884 publication date." He handed it to Babson. "You might want to put this in your library, to protect it."

"I will," Babson said. He opened the book. "This is marvelous. Thank you for pointing it out to us."

He turned to me. "You'll look through the rest of the books, Steve? See if there are any others that belong in the library?"

"Of course." Rochester sat on his haunches beside Macarius, but he was more interested in nosing a book on the shelf. "What's there, boy?" I asked him.

I picked up the book he had indicated, which had a similar binding to those around it. Old leather, with gold letters inscribed on it. But it had a different title: *The Royal Danish Arabia Expedition*.

"I bet this is the book missing from the museum," I said. "Hiding in plain sight all along."

"You'd better hold onto that for safe keeping," Babson said. "Can you arrange to get it to the FBI for verification?"

"I'll call Agent Quillian," I said.

We walked outside, and Babson left with the old Book of Hours. I held onto the Expedition book while talking with students and nibbling a few sugar cookies. Rochester got a couple of those, too, from me and from students.

Lori and Deana left with the last of the students, and Joey and I watched Macarius drive his van full of computers back to New York.

"Heck of a week," Joey said.

"Between River Bend and here, I'd say it's been a heck of two weeks," I said. With Rochester by my side I went back to my office and called Hank Quillian.

"Where did you find it?" he asked, after I told him I had the missing book in my possession.

"In a bookshelf of old prayerbooks," I said. "It has a similar binding to the books it was with, which may be why your agents didn't find it."

"And the dog didn't sniff it either."

I was about to argue that Rochester had indeed sniffed the volume out, but then I realized he was speaking about Archie, who'd been specifically trained to follow the scent of ancient artifacts. "Yeah, that's probably right."

"I have to come out to Bucks County next week on another case, so I'll call you and make plans to hand over the book. Keep it safe until then."

I looked at Rochester, who grinned at me and then slumped to the floor. In one fluid movement he rolled onto his side, his legs out and his head down. He knew his work was finished and it was time for a rest.

Chapter 32

A Long Time

J oey and I locked up the property, and I took my dog home.

He got some extra treats that evening, for all the work he had done. Lili wasn't happy that he'd attacked Grantay, though. "You could have been shot, boy," she said. "You can't keep getting into trouble like that."

Then she looked up at me. "That goes for you, too, mister."

I kissed her. "I know. If we're going to get married, I need to stay in one piece. And Rochester, too."

"And Rochester, too," she echoed.

Lili and I enjoyed an indulgent weekend. We took Rochester far out into the country to a park where Lili wanted to take some photographs and he could run around like a maniac. Then we went over to Joey and Mark's for a spring barbecue, and Rochester drew on deep reserves of energy to chase Brody around the house.

Sunday afternoon we received an email from Henry Meskin. He was pleased to announce that a new manager had been appointed by Keystone Properties. Vinod Balakrishnan, an experienced association manager with several sets of initials after his name, would be joining us on Monday morning. Henry asked us to give Mr. Balakrishnan time to get oriented before besieging him with questions.

The second part of his email concerned the tree removal, which was starting the next morning. He listed the addresses where home-owners were requested to remove their vehicles to protect against falling branches.

"So your work on the tree committee is almost over," Lili said.

I shook my head. "Vic is starting on phase one of the removals, the trees that absolutely have to go. We have phase two after that. Then we'll have to buy new trees and have them planted and make sure they thrive. But I hope that will be less contentious."

Monday morning I woke to the distant sound of a chain saw. Rochester had his front paws up against the windowsill, looking out to Sarajevo Way.

I joined him there but I couldn't see anything nearby. "Come on, let's go see what we can find," I said to him. I pulled on a pair of jeans and a long-sleeved T, and he followed me downstairs.

I hooked his leash and we walked outside. It was a bright, sunny day, the sky a robin's egg blue, and everything was peaceful for a moment—until I heard the chainsaw again. We cut through a break in the townhouses to the street behind us, where I spotted a Tree-B-Gone truck.

Vic Davis was standing beside one of the trees that most needed to come down. It had been planted way too close to the street, and its roots were tearing up the pavement as well as the homeowner's drive-way. A guy in a bucket arm from the truck was up above us, slicing off branches.

A couple of neighbors were watching the action. It was sad to watch the magnificent oak get stripped of its adornment, leaving a forlorn trunk stretched against the sky. But it was necessary, and I consoled myself with the idea that there'd be a new tree there soon, back far enough from driveway and pavement.

It wouldn't provide shade for Rochester and me on our walks for a long time, but then, we weren't going anywhere.

Author's Notes

Thanks for reading. I'd love to stay in touch with you. Subscribe to one or more of my newsletters, Gay Mystery and Romance or Golden Retriever Mysteries and I promise I won't spam you!

Follow me at <u>Goodreads</u> to see what I'm reading, and my <u>author page</u> at Facebook where I post news and giveaways.

Did you miss something in The Golden Retriever Mysteries? You'll find the entire series here: https://amzn.to/3Kki7w6

Looking for something new to read?

Neil has a series just for you!

Mahu Investigations:
You'll fall instantly in love with Kimo, from his scrupulous approach to his job to his easy way with his nieces, nephews, brothers, and friends, even when some turn against him on his new path. What's happening to him is the late-breaking realization that he's gay. If he's going to accept that and live as he's meant to, he has to upend everything and learn a whole new culture. It's a rocky path, and that's what makes a good story. Author Plakcy, creator of The Golden Retriever Mysteries, weaves a very different kind of tale here —realistic and hard-boiled, yet also empathetic and warm. **MAHU is a taut, ingenious, many-threaded mystery, each unexpected plot twist leading believably to the next, yet nothing telegraphed—in other words, an extremely satisfying read.**

The entire series is here: https://amzn.to/3Gokhsa
Author of over 50 romance and mystery novels and short story

collections. **Neil's entire catalog of books are here:** https://amzn.to/3I7qOIf

About the Author

NEIL S. PLAKCY is the author of over fifty mystery and romance novels, including the best-selling golden retriever mysteries and the highly acclaimed *Mahu* series, a three-time finalist for the Lambda Literary Awards. His stories have been featured in numerous venues, including the Bouchercon anthology <u>Florida Happens</u> and Malice Domestic's <u>Murder Most Conventional</u> and several Happy Homicides collections.

He is a professor of English at Broward College in South Florida, where he lives with his husband and their rambunctious golden retrievers.

His website is <u>www.mahubooks.com</u>.

Ingram Content Group UK Ltd.
Milton Keynes UK
UKHW040803240723
425668UK00001B/104